MW01492018

ROXANE
GAY
BO□KS

Also by Sara Levine

Treasure Island!!!

Short Dark Oracles

THE
HITCH

THE
HITCH

A NOVEL

SARA LEVINE

ROXANE
GAY
BOOKS

New York

FIRST EDITION

Printed in the United States of America

This book's interior was designed by Norman E. Tuttle
at Alpha Design & Composition.
This book is set in 12-pt. Bembo Std at Alpha Design & Composition
of Pittsfield, NH.

First Grove Atlantic hardcover edition: January 2026

Library of Congress Cataloging-in-Publication data is available for this title.

ISBN 978-0-801-6592-3
eISBN 978-0-8021-6593-0

Roxane Gay Books
an imprint of Grove Atlantic
154 West 14th Street
New York, NY 10011

Distributed by Publishers Group West

groveatlantic.com

26 27 28 29   10 9 8 7 6 5 4 3 2 1

For Chris and Sally

Do not feel lonely,
the entire universe is inside you.

—Rumi

PART ONE

Chapter 1

They dropped him off on a cold Saturday morning in February.

He was six years old. I never wanted children, not for one atom-splitting second, but my nephew I adored. Especially since he'd gotten out of diapers. They live two miles away, but mostly I saw him on Saturdays, partly because his mother threw him into a river of activities. Soccer, tae kwon do, swimming; after which she dredged up his body and dragged him to paintball fields, batting cages, trampoline parks. "She can't sit still in a room with him," I told Victor. I didn't like it. I didn't like how they were raising him. Every Saturday I hosted him from ten to twelve and gladly would have kept him longer (lunch, dinner, overnight), but they whisked him back again, as if he were on a timer. They were controlling, I said.

She was controlling.

But that Saturday his parents didn't do the usual drop-off. They were headed to Mexico, and Nathan would stay with me for seven nights. Eight days! A whole week with Nathan, just me and that golden boy.

But the drop-off? It took forever! First off, Astrid wouldn't come all the way in, just stood there looking at Walter like she expected him to knock her over and plant his forepaws on her chest. Walter is a Newfoundland, and Newfs, as you probably know, are nicknamed the nanny dog. They're famously sweet. But Astrid isn't a dog person. Or a cat person. Or a people person. Holy cannoli, she and Victor said when I got Walter. If I wanted a dog, I might have begun with a smaller breed, one that wouldn't need so much exercise or grooming. A Chihuahua, or a bulldog, possibly a pug.

"Cute now, but he'll grow big as a fucking pony," Victor said.

"Please don't think we're going to help out. We already have a child," by which Astrid meant, We already have a vampire, draining my maternal heart. "Change your mind and you can take him to the shelter."

Walter is gorgeous; except for a minor incongruity in his forelegs, a perfect specimen. The minute he pressed his large-domed head against my thigh, I loved him to the point of lunacy. Even when he peed on the rug and slung tangles of fur and drool on the wall, I didn't think, My sister-in-law's right, dogs are a lot of work, I should take him to the shelter. No, I thought, this dog is magic: He's steady and loyal and blunt-nosed and black—black like a bear—with fur so deep I can lose my fingers in it.

Unlike his parents, Nathan understood us from the start. He could pull Walter's tail, snatch a toy, eat a dripping ice cream cone at mandibular height: Walter never growled. They were like brothers. That first summer, we followed the two of them out into the yard, and I shouted out, "They're like twinned lambs that did frisk i' the sun. And bleat the one at th' other!"

"Shakespeare," Victor said to his blank-faced wife. She isn't much of a reader. "I think that dog could use more training."

"We *all* could use more training." I clicked my tongue. "Lie down, Walter. Lie down. Lie down! See?"

Astrid rolled her eyes. "You shouldn't have to say it six times."

"I said it three times."

"Who's counting?" Victor said diplomatically.

She is, I thought. Astrid took my brother's elbow and walked him around the crabapple tree, whispering, while Nathan and I ran our hands all over Walter's belly. The backyard is eight hundred square feet, but I'd never bothered to landscape, which was just as well—Walter would have room to run. The grass was a mess of chickweed, wild violets, and knotweed, a fact I noticed only for the first time that summer. I paid someone to dig up the scraggly bushes and put up a six-foot fence of sustainably forested Western red cedar, which smelled terrific. But I never succeeded in getting rid of the burdock. With large, hairy leaves and prickly burs, the burdock sprang up after the fence was erected, and grew so aggressively it buckled the slats.

"Your plants are creeping over into the neighbor's yard," Astrid told me. Her tone suggested I was creeping, not nature.

Chapter 2

I was still adjusting to my brother's marriage. Maybe I still am. He and Astrid met on a Panama Canal cruise. They married three months after they met—county clerk, no guests allowed—bought a house they couldn't afford, and produced a child as if picking one more feature: We'll have granite countertops and, oh yes, a baby boy. That's how they roll. No forethought. Make it up as you go along.

Of course, I'm the opposite. I overthink, but I accomplish. When our parents died (heart disease, breast cancer), I'd only done half a year at Vassar. But I moved back to Chicago, transferred to UIC, and kept an eye on Victor while he finished high school. I got us out of the dim, airless house in which we grew up and started an artisanal yogurt business. I kept Victor from selling running shoes the rest of his life.

He's a podiatrist now and makes good money.

But I was telling you about the drop-off. They rang the bell, and Walter began barking and spinning in excited circles. At the threshold I high-fived Nathan and obliged Astrid by hanging on to Walter's collar (white faux leather, brass studs). "Sweetie, careful!" Astrid said when Nathan raked a hand across Walter's head. Please trot down the hall, I said over the barking, and check out Nathan's room.

Just that morning my friend Omar had helped me hang a pair of vintage tennis rackets and style the bookshelf. *The Encyclopedia of Animals* looked fabulous alongside a large gleaming N (salvaged from a marquee) and a treasured photo of Nathan nuzzling Walter. Every detail was enchanting to ponder; after Omar left, I impregnated a glass apothecary jar with saltwater taffy and twice changed the position of the rug. Aglow, I watched as Nathan toured his quarters—patting the mushroom-shaped lamp, unearthing the yo-yo I'd whimsically tucked beneath his pillow—but his parents were indifferent. Under her winter coat, Astrid had dressed for Cancún and was worked up lest Walter drool on her jumpsuit. Now and then she reminded Nathan where she'd packed pajamas and melatonin, as if he and I were complete idiots and wouldn't be able to find our way around a duffel bag. Victor dashed back to the car for a grubby booster seat and, colliding with Walter, scolded him for nosing his crotch.

"Everyone calls a boisterous yellow Lab a family dog," I said. "But when a *black* dog bounces or slobbers or barks, people shrink back like he's Cerberus at the gates of hell. Have you ever noticed that?"

Colorism was not a familiar concept to them. Unpacking, Astrid held up a stuffed toy. "This is Whippy," she said. "Please put Whippy on a high shelf."

"Wonderful Whippy!" Nathan said automatically, but his glance skipped from the saggy rabbit back to Walter, whose vigorous bulk he chased around the coffee table, laughing and shrieking when somebody's energetic tail knocked over my Alexander Girard collection. I smiled and set the wooden dolls upright. You have to relax when it comes to dogs. Otherwise where's the joy?

"Walter's all right," Omar likes to say. "He's just a hundred and fifty pounds of chaos."

By chaos he meant fun.

Chapter 3

When Victor and Astrid first decided to go to Mexico, they didn't tell me. Nathan leaked the plan during one of our Saturday afternoons, and I waited until Victor and I went to the pancake house to address it.

"I heard you guys are going to Mexico in February."

"Just for a week."

"Without Nathan?"

"Yeah, he's going to stay with his friend Tommy."

"ADHD Tommy whose mother runs a flavored popcorn business out of her basement?"

"Tommy Bessinger. His mother's a food entrepreneur. Like you."

"I did six million in sales last quarter, but never mind."

"Well, the Bessingers have three boys—"

"That sounds unpleasant."

"—and those big-family vibes will be fun for Nathan. Plus, it's easy for them to get him to school."

"Maybe you haven't clocked it, but I live eleven minutes from Nathan's school. And I'd love to take him to the symphony. They're doing Mahler 7."

"He'd probably prefer the dentist."

"Two full stacks!" the waiter boomed. "One side of sausage and bacon!"

"No meat for me," I said and blocked the descending plate as deftly as a martial artist. Victor took his food, beaming. He loved this restaurant because our parents had loved it, and our parents hardly knew what a restaurant was. They'd been afraid of restaurants, I said, which is why they only ever took us to the pancake house or McDonald's. Twenty-five years ago, McDonald's was already an environmental disaster, but our parents ignored the clamshell controversy and kept on eating Big Macs laced with toxic styrene. Victor was stuck in a rut, liking the same food our parents did, even though it was heart attack food and contributed to their early deaths.

"Not Mom," Victor said. "Pancakes don't cause cancer."

"They haven't yet done the studies."

My pancakes were the size of wagon wheels and tasted like a sponge you find out in the road.

"Did you read the *National Geographic* article I sent you about the history of pancakes?" I asked.

"No," Victor said.

In a glacier, in a crevasse, in the Italian Alps, archeologists had found a mummy with einkorn flour in its

stomach and now they were claiming The Pancake went
back to the Ice Age.

"Einkorn flour and ferns," I said. "Is that a pancake?
Maybe a savory fritter. And why do we need ridiculously
broad transhistorical arguments on behalf of pancakes? It's
bad enough people build 'houses' around them."

"Hey, what's happening with Cultured Cow?"

"I'm negotiating the buyout."

"And?"

And, I said, ignoring him, people who trace the
pancake back to the Ice Age are trying to deny the pancake's place in American history. Did he know Thomas
Jefferson was obsessed with innovating the pancake at
Monticello?

No, Victor said, looking around for the waiter, but
I found myself unable to stop talking about Jefferson's
pancake-making slaves, even as I sensed I was losing him.
I could've told him that by parking Nathan with the Bessingers, he'd wounded me, but instead I said, in a pierc-
ing voice, that the Aunt Jemima logo was inspired by a
minstrel song.

Soon enough the waiter brought the bill, and I
plucked it up before Victor could pay it, and as I paid,
I tried to make a connection between white America's
love of pancakes and the way slavery had slowly evolved
into the mass incarceration of Black people. That's why
Aunt Jemima pancakes are so popular, I said, popular

with white people, even the ones who don't go to pancake houses but stay at home and make pancakes from a Quaker Oats box mix. Isn't that ironic? While Thomas Jefferson's slaves were grinding buckwheat for his so-called elevated pancakes, Quakers were agitating against slavery. Only a fool would make a love match out of Quakers and Aunt Jemima, I said, but America is filled with fools, and of course American food conglomerates have no shame.

The waiter brought me my change.

Nothing improved when Pepsi bought Quaker Oats, I said, pocketing my change, they continue to push out a totally reprehensible line of products as if the Thirteenth Amendment had never happened. They took the rag off Aunt Jemima's head and gave her a pair of pearl earrings as if Aunt Jemima only needed a makeover. Do they think people are stupid? I said as Victor and I rose from the sticky table and headed for the door. Unfortunately, people are stupid, I said. Every few years a Black person publishes an editorial in the newspaper calling for the end of Aunt Jemima, once and for all, and it's like this person is talking into a well. A Black person publishes an editorial in the newspaper and it's like this person is talking from a glacier in a gully in the Italian Alps. A Black person may as well be the Iceman who has been dead for five thousand years because nobody can hear this person. Meanwhile in the same newspaper, a white person publishes an editorial about a low-carb diet and there will be two thousand enthusiastic comments.

Victor and I stood in the slush-covered parking lot between my BMW and his Chrysler.

He said, "I gather you're upset we didn't ask you to look after Nathan while we go to Mexico."

Chapter 4

"Why are they even going to Mexico?" Omar said the next day.

He was in Vegas for the week, and the noise of the trade show thrummed behind him.

"I don't know, I didn't ask him. Selling lots of wetsuits?"

"Not really, but remember the scuba cylinder that ruptured last year at Mermet Springs? Last night I met the guy who manufactures it. They're mired in a horrible lawsuit."

"Did you sleep with him?"

"I just met him, and I think he's straight."

"You're in Vegas."

"You're in Evanston. What are you doing?"

"Wishing I could look after Nathan for that week in February."

"Rose, you see him every Saturday."

"For two measly hours."

"What's happening with the buyout?"

"Due diligence. I should be free by March."

"Everything's coming up Roses," quipped Omar, not for the first time. His Ethel Merman impersonation led to my Ethel Merman impersonation, which led to a discussion of how Ethel Merman died. Cancer? Brain tumor?

"Brain cancer," I decided. "Speaking of sickness, last night I found a PubMed study on the link between boyhood ADHD and adult criminality. Remember ADHD Tommy? I think Victor and Astrid should know."

Omar said he had to go. The cephalopod presentation was starting.

Chapter 5

I never did send Victor and Astrid the article about ADHD. A few days later, Victor called—without any pressure from me—and said they changed their minds. I could host Nathan in February, provided I understood the rules and didn't do anything extra, like take him to the symphony, or buy him an Xbox.

"I don't know what an Xbox is," I said truthfully.

"Rose."

"All right, I'll give Omar the symphony tickets."

"Routine. Bedtime, meals, homework. Accountability at school is an issue."

"Did you read that article I sent from *The Atlantic* about unconscious gender bias? Teachers grind down the boys, starting in kindergarten."

"Ms. Shingler gives ten minutes of homework. Just make sure he does it."

"Of course. I'm not like Mom. Remember when you begged her to let you quit swim class? Because you were scared of Mr. Norris."

"I had eczema. It was the chlorine."

"It was Mom being wishy-washy. How's your crawl? Can you even butterfly?"

"Never mind," Victor said. "Just make sure Nathan sticks to his routine."

I began to plan meals. I love planning meals. In my twenties, I had an obsession with Mollie Katzen and the Moosewood Collective. Not that I joined the Collective—or ever visited the restaurant—but I believed in Mollie Katzen, particularly her cookbook *The Enchanted Broccoli Forest*, and threw myself into making healthy meals out of vegetables, grains, and dairy. For reasons I can no longer fathom, I was particularly keen on serving friends the Moosewood Mushroom Yogurt Pie with Spinach Crust. I also remember a socially strained dinner party at which I served crumbling tofu burgers, baked not fried, in an apartment that had no dining room table; I expected people to eat them in their laps. It was precisely at the height of my fervent *Enchanted Broccoli Forest* phase that I started an artisanal yogurt business, believing yogurt was a health food. In fact, I used the life insurance money from my parents to launch The Cultured Cow. For years we only made three flavors—Plain Jane, Vanilla Has Bean, and Coco Loco—and they were exquisite: handmade, hand-strained, hand-packed. We developed a small but fanatical following.

And then I read *The China Study: The Most Comprehensive Study of Nutrition Ever Conducted,* which posits a link between animal products and heart disease, diabetes, and cancer. No more cheesecake with yogurt, I decided. No more blintzes and kreplach. How could I pretend yogurt was a health food when it was a high-calorie, high-sugar product with the nutritional content of pudding? And don't even get me started on the environmental angles. I wanted wholeheartedly to be a vegan. I practically was a vegan, except for the fact that I'd tied my livelihood to the dairy industry and occasionally ate pancakes with my brother.

Here's a great way to make vegan pizza. Slice five yellow onions—three-eighths of an inch wide. Heat a tablespoon of olive oil in a skillet, add onions, cover, and cook at low heat. As the humble plant takes on the color of bourbon, exult. Obviously it's not cheese; it's caramelized onions. But the flavor's so rich you'll stop missing that thick, viscous layer of mozzarella that's probably going to give you, at the least, arthritis. My father loved pizza and died of heart disease, age forty-eight.

The meal planning project buoyed me, especially as the days were getting darker and colder, and my work life sucked. Doug D'Andrea was the only employee who knew I was selling the company, because I needed him to do things, and I'd started avoiding staff. Sylvia Klausner or Bill Whitaker would hover in the doorway, saying something about pints, wholesale tubs, and mix, and I'd shoo them away. Instead of holding meetings, I emailed. Omar said I was "isolating."

Meanwhile we were launching a green tea yogurt. It was terrible timing, but I thought it would be easier to sell a business that was expanding. I even hired a social media manager to make a ballyhoo about the new flavor. Becca was so young she didn't know the word "ballyhoo," so I stopped giving her directives that sounded like I lived in 1901. The campaign rolled on.

> Gotcha Matcha!
> I eat it at my dacha.
> With a squirt of sriracha.
> While I'm dancing the cha-cha.

"Why's it green?" Nathan asked.

"Green tea is trending. It's got antioxidants. I don't know, don't eat it, just give it to your mother."

Can you be joyed? Or only overjoyed? After Victor moved out, I'd turned his room into a study, which had actually become a dumping ground for household supplies. Now I cleaned it up and began to dream. I was so happy I'd been allotted a larger role than Saturday aunt. I browsed Pinterest, started a design binder. At antique shops, instead of scanning for midcentury ceramics, I thought, Well, what would Nathan like? I bought sample sizes of high-performance milk paint and slapped a gorgeous inky blue on the wall so I could see the hue in different lights.

"Too sober for a boy's room?" I asked Victor when I dropped by.

We faced each other in the doorway, him in baggy sweats and smudged glasses; me, smartly dressed, well-intentioned, armed with paint chips.

"I'm also considering yellow. Not the sickly eggnog of a baby's room, or the garish yellow of a sunflower. This mid-tone muted custard. Do you remember when Mom and Dad went to Atlanta for Cousin Ricky's wedding and left us with Aunt Edith and Uncle Al, whom we hardly knew? You and I slept on a cot in this dark, wood-paneled den where there was a paint-by-numbers oil of a weeping clown, which scared us so badly Aunt Edith came and took it off the wall. That clown had yellow ruffles. So maybe not yellow."

"Why are you here?" he said. "I'd appreciate if you call first. Boundaries."

"You're always welcome to drop by *my* house," I said, squeezing past. "I just want to pop into Nathan's room and see what's going on in terms of color."

In a flash I was upstairs, but I'd forgotten: Every room in their house is painted white. It had been painted white before they moved in. In Nathan's room, the walls were not only white but bare—even though I'd given him a gorgeous reproduction of Landseer's *Saved* painting, the one with a Newfie panting over a half-drowned girl he's rescued from the sea.

The frame alone cost six hundred dollars.

"Can you believe it?" I said that night to Omar on the phone. "A museum-quality, hand-painted replica. And it was nowhere in sight. Astrid must have sold the painting on eBay or shoved it in the closet—anything to restore the house's arctic barrenness."

"Hold on," Omar said. "Someone on line two. Frogman. Hello?"

"It's still me."

"Hello? Hello?"

"Omar, it's me."

"They hung up, I guess."

"They make no effort on that house. It's not the white walls, it's the passivity that's baffling."

"And the rest of the conversation?"

"What conversation? Astrid barely said hello when she came home. Just sank into a chair and began bitching about the bunionectomy. How Victor's colleague overcorrected her big toe, it didn't heal right, I forget the details exactly. The whole time I was staring at their walls and thinking, White! Why so white? I mean, neutrals can be nice, but the way they cling to white feels almost racially motivated. *You* understand; you're half Mexican."

"There's someone on line two," Omar said.

* * *

To think I might have been like them! I might have been so afraid to make a mark, I didn't dare open a pot of paint. But in the stale breath of their indifference, I kept on planning Nathan's room. Inky blue seemed better for an accent wall or the back of a bookshelf, and yellow too reminiscent of weeping clown. Finally, after hours of unrestrained surfing, I discovered a British paint company offering a color named Wevet, which means spiderweb in Dorset. Almost white with a hint of grey.

The color worked well with my house's palette: mascarpone, vert de terre, cooking apple green. Blue was sober; yellow, scary; Wevet, neutral as a spiderweb. Obviously I was making Nathan a room, not a spiderweb, but Omar liked the Wevet and I liked the Wevet. So in early January, I found the Michelangelo of house painters, who, for a small fortune, came and painted the room.

On the first coat, the color was an austere, almost churchly white. But the following Saturday when Nathan looked at it, he said, "It's grey. Like the color of sweat socks." In fact, he began to call it the sweat sock room, which shows how clever he is but also that he didn't understand the enormous effort I had put into making him a sanctuary.

Chapter 6

Neither did Astrid.

"I heard you're painting and buying furniture," she said a few days later. "Don't do that. He's six. He can sleep on your couch."

"You can't put a kid on a Louis XV sofa for seven nights. Cabriole legs and a cartouche back?"

"Then put him in a sleeping bag. You don't need to spoil him," by which she meant, Please make him sleep on the floor, and carry firewood, and scrape turnips, and pick wantonly scattered lentils and peas out of the ashes. It was a mother's job to spoil him, whereas a stay at my house had to be grim as a fairy tale so Nathan wouldn't grow fond.

"He doesn't need a color scheme. He doesn't need a bamboo bedframe and nightstand. He's a kid, Rose. Please don't make it the Taj Mahal."

Only a person who buys all her furniture from Craigslist would think I was making the Taj Mahal. A year ago, for our special Saturdays, I'd bought Nathan magnetic blocks sourced from a sustainable wood cooperative in Honduras. Astrid objected to that too, probably because Nathan liked them more than her plastic Target junk.

But I don't want to string this story out. My point is, they did not trust me. Which is why, the Saturday morning they dropped him off, they hovered. They wouldn't sit down. But they hung around so long Nathan needed snacks.

"Hey, Aunt Rose," he said, holding a glass of apple juice and chewing popcorn. "How'm I going to get to school this week? You don't know where Rawlings is."

"Of course I do. Last year. Share Your Heritage Day. Remember I brought bagels and talked about Jewish holidays?"

He gave me a blank look. But he didn't remember his heritage either. Sometimes Victor and Astrid called him a Cashew: part Catholic, part Jewish. Pure nut, his mother added.

"Oh yeah, I remember. You got a ticket 'cause you parked in the bus lane! You were mad it was a hundred and ten dollars! And you brought that weird tofu cream cheese. And Trinity Johnson kept saying tofu cream cheese tastes like cat butt!"

"All right," I said, "that's enough of memory lane."

"And when Trinity's mom brought cupcakes with Funfetti frosting, I got to have chocolate *and* vanilla!"

"That's nice, but what's her heritage, juvenile diabetes?" My cell phone bleated. "Excuse me."

I stepped out of the room. All week I'd been playing phone tag with the lawyer and expected good news. By which I mean the news I'd sold The Cultured Cow.

But this was bad news: The buyer had walked.

Someone sluiced my veins with cold water. Then I went back into the living room and said:

"Well, it's nothing. Just the deal collapsed."

"Whoops," Astrid said.

"Sorry, Sis."

"That's okay," I said. That's how I handled disappointment: lock it up and swallow the key. "Anyway, you better catch your plane."

"Do you want to quickly tell us what happened?" Victor asked.

"It didn't happen."

"Tell us."

"She doesn't have to tell us," Astrid said.

"The intricacies of selling a small business are difficult to explain."

"Come on!"

"Well, this jerk—"

"Is this the intricate part?" Astrid said.

"—was pre-approved for a business acquisition loan. I gave him six months to examine the books, but now his financing's collapsed."

"Bad luck," Victor said.

"Can Walter eat popcorn?" Nathan asked.

"Victor, come on. We need to catch our flight."

I took away Nathan's apple juice so he could hug his mother. Then Victor hugged him, then they both hugged him, then Victor stepped away so Astrid could hug Nathan again, as if they were filming *Sophie's Choice* and she'd just elected to send him to the gas chamber. Possibly I was more ill-tempered than usual because I had just failed to sell my business for twelve million dollars. A few more words were exchanged about practical matters (FaceTime, bedtime, toothbrush), after which I delicately nudged them to the door, where they began, against all rational expectations, to hug again. Even when the door was open, they didn't walk through it and drive to the airport. Instead, Astrid turned to Victor and said:

"Wow, it feels so weird! I've never left him."

"It's only eight days."

"I know."

"And he's in good hands."

"I know. I just . . . I just have a bad feeling."

You are the bad feeling, I thought, rather uncharitably, and wished we'd talked in advance about how they were going to drop him off, since they seemed not to grasp that the best thing for Nathan was for them to just leave.

Finally, they walked to their car and left.

Chapter 7

The first thing I did was scurry into the Wevet room and get the gift, exquisitely wrapped and hidden from Nathan for months, despite a temptation to say screw-it-all and lavish it on him early. "Surprise!" Nathan's eyes lit up and he tugged at the wide silk ribbon. He would be blue and I would be white, I thought, or I would be blue and he would be white. But when Nathan pulled the alabaster chess set out of the box, he said, "Oh, that," and cast around for something else to play with.

His father, I soon learned, had hinted I might give him a chess set. But had the spoilsport, I mean your dad, hinted the chess set was a collector's item, celestially hued, handcrafted in Italy? I tried to laugh off my disappointment, but I felt annoyed—and slightly demented because I'd forgotten I'd ever mentioned the chess set to Victor. When had I even *seen* him to tell him? Then I remembered an unhappy day in December when Victor and I had gone to lunch at The Grüne Tavern.

The Grüne is a long, low-ceilinged room with dark wood tables, red-checked cloths, and heavy tableware. The walls are barnacled with wine casks and cuckoo clocks. The waitresses wear green dirndls, and the place is defiantly meat-minded. Beef broth, steak filled with ham and cheese, broccoli with ham. It turned out Astrid had recommended the place.

Victor ordered a winter beer, Bratknödel, and Wiener schnitzel while I scanned the menu, which read like an insult too subtle for Victor to catch. Did he *know* 99 percent of Austrians voted in support of the union with Germany? Reluctantly, I ordered the house salad with schnitzel and asked to hold the schnitzel.

The waitress cast doubt on my choice. "We're famous for our schnitzel."

"And Vienna was famous for its Jews before Anschluss. Sigmund Freud, Karl Kraus, Victor Adler, Arthur—"

"I'll have her schnitzel," Victor said hurriedly. "Just put it on the side. Please and thanks!" he called out to the waitress's back.

"Was I rude? This place puts me on edge."

"It's not the pancake house."

It certainly was not the pancake house, and maybe Victor truly thought I'd like the Austrian restaurant. Because he liked it. When the waitress delivered his Bratknödel, he cried out joyfully, "What've we got here?" and I cried out, "Three different animal life-forms ground up into a meatball!" Then we laughed and changed the subject.

This is probably when I told Victor I'd won the alabaster chess set in an online auction. I don't remember. What I do remember is Victor's unusual chattiness. First, he only rambled on about the weather: snow tonight, snow tomorrow. Second beer arriving, his range of observation widened. Astrid felt the cold, he confided. Their house was hard to heat. There's only so much long underwear can do. And that's why they decided to go to Mexico for a week—because he was tired of her complaining she was cold all the time, though he didn't say it in those words.

What he said was, having grown up in Chicago, he always told Astrid, who grew up in Florida, it wasn't so bad, but lately—slugging his beer—he'd begun to feel it was pretty bad, maybe the windchill and subzero temperatures and sludge and snow, the way your face got chapped while you shoveled, and the long, dark, endless afternoons, were intolerable and he'd never allowed himself to really feel them before, before Astrid. He was drunk now, that was obvious. Ashkenazi gene.

"It's three to five months, Vic. Suck it up. The rest of the year is beautiful."

"But I've never lived anywhere but the Midwest. Why not—why not enjoy—"

"Wiener schnitzel!" the waitress interrupted, as if she were surprised, indeed as if she had just been shot, "and for you, Haussalt mit Schnitzelstreifen, kein Schnitzel!"—then she glided away, oblivious to whose nerves she had shattered.

"Why not enjoy what?" I probed my salad; no meat clung to the underside of the lettuce.

"A temperate climate."

I scoffed. "You can't be serious."

But he was serious, or rather Astrid was serious. He confided she'd been looking online at real estate in Maui. My brother's not a beach person, he hates the feeling of sand between his toes and is overwhelmed by the way sand gets in the car. The last time he took Nathan swimming in Lake Michigan, he saw snails in the water and his skin itched for a week. As a child he had a terrible time eating barbecue chicken because he was afraid of getting sauce on his fingers. How could a person who was afraid of getting sauce on his fingers live in Hawaii? There would be sand, there would be sauce, there would be breezes blowing microscopic particulate matter into his sensitive sinuses. Of course, there would also be waterfalls and bamboo forests and stunning sunrises—but Victor never cared a fig for natural beauty. He relaxes by going to Costco. I pushed away my salad and tottered to the bathroom.

And when would I see Nathan?

In the Damentoilette I splashed cold water on my face and rested on a ridiculous Bavarian chair. I lingered so long Victor might have thought, My sister is unwell, my sister who practically raised me since I was sixteen, but instead he thought, I'll use this time to order dessert.

The waitress dropped the plate of deep-fried dumplings onto the table ("Your Töpfenknodel!") like she was spitting a curse.

"Victor, you can't move to Maui. Your practice is here."

True, he said, but his practice bored him. Heel pain, hammertoes, arthritis. He wanted to do something creative. And ever since Dr. Bromberger botched Astrid's bunionectomy, they'd been thinking how she could have avoided surgery.

"Wear sensible shoes," I said.

"Exactly. But a fashion-conscious woman doesn't want to wear ugly orthopedics."

"Is Astrid fashion-conscious?"

"Listen, she started drawing sandals. And we got an idea"—his cheeks aflame, he turned his flagon round and round—"to make our own line. The kind of shoes women would *like* to wear."

"Astrid majored in sports management at the University of Central Florida. People *train* for product design. They study textiles, or fashion—"

"I'm a DPM, and Astrid knows the consumer angle. You don't have to be a specialist." His eyes flashed behind his smudged glasses. "The woman who invented Spanx never worked in the garment industry. She sold fax machines. One day she got fed up with her pantyhose and cut off the feet. Voila! Ten years later she sold the business for a billion dollars."

"That's a fairy tale, Victor. For every Sara Blakely there are ten thousand failed entrepreneurs."

"You know her?"

"Not personally. But everyone knows that story."

Victor stared moodily at his Töpfenknodel.

"You need a business plan. Nobody in their right mind moves to Hawaii to start a business. Do you realize how expensive things are once you leave the mainland?" I laughed without mirth. "Probably not, since I paid your way through podiatry school and helped finance your house."

Victor's ears grew pink. "We're excited. We'll learn by doing. Didn't you learn by doing?"

"Yes," I said. "And I dream of undoing what I did."

Chapter 8

That was December, but now it was February and I had Nathan all to myself. The chess set had been given, Walter had eaten the wrapping paper, Nathan had tied the silk ribbon around Walter's tail. We were alone, we could do whatever we wanted! Stop combing the filthy fur of the past, I thought and ushered Nathan into the kitchen.

People think vegans eat only salad, but I recommend a wholesome hot lunch, especially on a cold February day. Here's a favorite: Cream of Tomato Soup. Smash ten garlic cloves and heat until golden brown in a tablespoon of olive oil. Add a teaspoon of red pepper flakes, two tablespoons of tomato paste, and stir. Throw in two cans of white beans and a big can of crushed tomatoes. Bring to a low boil, then simmer until slightly thickened and fragrant. (We played with Walter forty minutes.) Once the soup tastes rich, let your favorite six-year-old boy smash half of the beans with the back of a wooden spoon. Add a teaspoon or two of maple syrup and a can of coconut milk. Eat with a good, crusty bread. Delicious! Nobody misses the traditional, artery-clogging cream.

Nathan ate two bowls and then sprawled on the living room rug, marching a blue rook over Walter's mounded back.

After the Austrian restaurant, I enjoyed my Saturdays with Nathan, but in my more paranoid moments I suspected Victor and Astrid were using this time to lay the foundation of the new life that would exclude me. The week of Christmas, Astrid canceled my Saturday by text. Nathan was going to the trampoline park in Elmhurst with Tommy Bessinger: "Last-minute switcheroo. Boys need to off-load some energy." Wounded, I put the glockenspiel I'd bought in a gift bag and drove to their house.

In the window I saw a heavily trimmed Christmas tree I could have helped decorate. I twitched with envy. If they'd asked, I would have brought a garland of dried orange slices. Cinnamon cookies. Plant-based candles.

I left the glockenspiel on their doorstep.

Walter and I spent Christmas Day alone. Nor did we observe Hanukkah, unless you count my impulsive purchase of a dog cookie iced with the word "Chewish."

"Maybe we should've had a holiday party," Doug D'Andrea remarked as we went over the sales returns. "It might improve morale around here."

I told him holiday parties were microaggressions. People had time off if they wanted it. I hoped he and John had a nice holiday.

"Eric," he said after a moment of confusion. "But yeah, thanks."

At some point, in the midst of my holiday funk, it dawned on me they'd chosen, for their trip to Mexico, an all-inclusive mega-resort on the beach of Cancún, owned by a disreputable Spanish hotel chain, notorious for trying to build a fourteen-hundred-room beachfront resort on a turtle sanctuary.

Thank goodness the environmentalists won that battle! On Tripadvisor I found Glen A. of Parsippany, New Jersey, complaining he'd had to pay eighty-four pesos to enter the protected beach, and Karla M. of Valparaiso, Indiana, outraged her party had been told they couldn't bring alcohol or cigarettes; soon it would be Astrid C. bitching she preferred the zip line. It was lucky Doug D'Andrea knocked on my door to troubleshoot a recurrent problem with our HVAC/refrigeration system, or I might have spent another hour on the internet fuming.

"If you go to that resort," I told Astrid when she dropped Nathan off the next Saturday morning (lately they dropped him off like a parcel, but this time I pulled on my coat and boots and came out to the car), "you'll miss the real flavor of Mexico. You should try San Cristóbal or Jalisco or any of the less developed fishing villages in the Yucatán. Did you know your hotel sponsors dolphin rides that wreck the coral reef?"

"Belated Merry Christmas, Rose." She handed me a bottle of wine—exactly what she'd want to receive. Maybe one she had received. "They bump into the coral?"

"The dolphins? No, their feces breed algae. I'll send you—"

"Don't bother. I read on Facebook they have STIs, and anyway I'm too tired. I'd rather lie on the beach than swim with dolphins."

Walter bounded up to say hello, and there was a very friendly flurry, which Astrid immediately spoiled by saying Walter's claws had scratched her car door. It was the lightest of marks.

"You can buff that out in three minutes with a chamois," I said.

A few days later I e-mailed suggestions of more interesting and ethical places to travel (hello, solar-powered hotel in Tulum!), which I suspect they deleted without opening. Then one Saturday in late January, Nathan and I sat in my living room with *The Nutter Butter Bible*, talking about where food comes from—not, I hinted, the grocery store. Walnuts: native to Persia but commercially cultivated in China. Almonds: farmed in California but actually native to Iran. Macadamias: come from Australia but grow mostly in Hawaii, and by the way, did Mommy and Daddy ever discuss Hawaii? Or talk about moving to Hawaii? Casually remark they'd like to visit Hawaii?

No, Nathan said, lazily flipping through the book, they were going to Mexico, remember? Mommy talked about it all the time.

"And Daddy?"

"He doesn't seem as excited about it."

No, he wouldn't be. His eczema was likely to flare; he'd fear jellyfish stings and stay in his room, reading. Or maybe he'd sit by the pool, in an unflattering broad brim hat with neck flaps, while Astrid got drunk alone at the swim-up bar.

"Did they show you where they're staying?"

He shook his head. No, they didn't talk about—

"Would you like to see it?"

As I unfolded the ecological disaster, Nathan sucked on his T-shirt collar and then, suitably sobered, took over my laptop and Googled animals. He knew exactly which ones lived in Mexico.

"See this whale shark! Whale sharks are long as a school bus! Some weigh twenty thousand pounds and have teeny-tiny teeth and people swim beside them but don't get eaten."

"I doubt your parents are going to swim with whale sharks. Your mom just wants to lie on the beach. Did you see the Jet Skis? They dump about four gallons of gas and oil in the water."

"If I went to Mexico, I could see manatees and sea turtles. And a chacalaca!"

"What's that?" (Always astonished by his vocabulary.)

It was a bird; he said the wonderful name for me two or three times as he explained birds were descended from dinosaurs, and dinosaurs were the oldest life-forms on earth, at which point, with the directness an intelligent boy deserves, I corrected him.

"The microbes came first. They were here for billions of years."

"Tommy says—"

"Tommy doesn't know. One day we'll zip off to Amsterdam, where they're building a microbe museum, and I'll show you zombie fungus under a microscope!"

"When?"

"As soon as it opens. I'm on the mailing list."

"Are there whale sharks in Amsterdam?"

"No, but you'll like the microbe museum, Nathan, and I'm not just saying that because I sell yogurt—"

"There's definitely whale sharks in Mexico, but Mommy says I can't go. She and Daddy fight too much, and Mommy says they need quality time."

I closed *The Nutter Butter Bible* and looked at him sideways. "Hello! Your mother told you that?"

He picked at the book's flaking spine. "Mommy says we don't have secrets in our family."

"The real secret is that every family has secrets. Have you ever heard your parents fighting?"

"Sure," he said offhandedly, "all the time."

I couldn't believe it. Later, as Nathan played with his magnetic blocks, the information that Victor and Astrid had been fighting bobbed up and down in my mind. I'd been so preoccupied by a sense of exclusion, I'd failed to see the cracks in the foundation. Victor and Astrid were coming up on seven years . . . Could they be grasping at straws? Let's move to Hawaii, let's start a shoe business, let's relax on a beach and forget we rushed into an ill-suited marriage! Maybe instead of confiding in me, Victor had withdrawn and put up a false front. Maybe he feared I'd say, I told you so. (I had told him so . . .) In any case, if a resort vacation was the last gasp of a dying marriage, I'd forgive its excesses. Let them fill the pockets of a multi-national corporation, drink unlimited alcohol, harass the dolphins, and bore each other silly until the truth swam up and stung them on the face. They should never have married in the first place.

"Aunt Rose." Nathan looked up from the spindly tower he was building on the rug. "Why are you smiling?"

Chapter 9

That was January, and now it was February. As much as it pleased me to see Nathan handle the chess set, my head was full of fumes. There I sat, drinking high mountain oolong tea, Nathan marching a blue rook over Walter's mounded back, and instead of appreciating the moment, I shared a bitter thought or two about the buyout. Honestly, I said, if I'd understood twenty years ago how hard it was to run an artisanal yogurt company, I wouldn't have started The Cow; I would have moved immediately to Paris and learned to design textiles.

"Why don't you just make vegan yogurt, Aunt Rose?"

"I want to do something new."

"Cows have four stomachs."

"Because it's not just the deal falling apart. It's what a yogurt business stands for."

"They fart so much it's killing the planet."

"And the need to align my values with my life. You're six, you don't know what I mean . . ."

"You hate your job?"

"I don't believe in the job. It doesn't matter how ethically I source the vanilla for Vanilla Has Bean or how many green tea antioxidants I add to Gotcha Matcha! if I'm throwing in my lot with all the big dairy schmucks who say dairy makes you thrive. It's a lie—a gigantic, decades-long, lobbyist-supported lie that goes down in this country like a greasy sausage Egg McMuffin. I don't want to be a part of it anymore."

"What's a schmuck?"

"Never mind."

Nathan played on as if I'd only remarked on the weather.

"I'm going to be a vet when I grow up," he volunteered after a pause. "I don't think I'll ever get sick of that. Do you, Aunt Rose?" I didn't answer. "They said no to a dog—and to a cat—but do you think my parents would let me get a grasshopper mouse?"

I slurped my tea. He repeated the question.

"A mouse? No." I laughed hoarsely. "With your parents, you'll be lucky to get a goldfish."

Despite the despair I felt about The Cultured Cow, that Saturday was the loveliest afternoon Nathan and I ever had. We had no idea what would befall us on Sunday, only the sense of a holiday unspooling. We played Bananagrams, walked Walter, played Boggle, put a bandana on Walter, attempted to play chess. Did he want to FaceTime his parents? Naaaaah, maybe tomorrow. Why had I doubted my ability to entertain him? He was easy. When it grew dark, I turned on all the lamps and said, "Pick a number." "Four," he said, and we played Mahler 4. For dinner I showed him how to pan-fry tempeh and string beans, and he was tucked under his poppy-bright bedspread by eight o'clock. "Goodness, when did it begin to snow?" I said as I closed the custom-made drapes on a storybook sky: thick white flakes swirling on black velvet.

We high-fived goodnight.

In the morning, the backyard was smooth and shiny, the crabapple tree, big with snow. Four inches! Delighted, we leashed Walter and trekked through a newly whitened world to the vegan bakery. The air was crisp, and the rooftops sparkled with frost.

"This is how to enjoy the Chicago winter," I said as we headed to the park, eating warm, flaky croissants straight out of the bag.

Nathan's small, bright voice rang out in the quiet.

The world belonged to us alone.

"Can I go pet it?"

In the middle of the field where Walter likes to run off-leash stood a woman in a faux-fur bucket hat with a small brown dog, whom Nathan mistook for a puppy.

On first sight all corgis look like puppies, because they're under thirty pounds and have short legs. Later we learned the dog was Walter's age, but Walter is only slightly longer than he is tall and tears across the field like a tiger, whereas when the corgi saw Nathan coming, she could only waddle forward. She wore a ridiculous pink rhinestone collar and she waddled forward, because the woman had her on a retractable leash.

Everyone knows a retractable leash is a disaster. A retractable leash is a danger to you, your dog, and everyone around you. If you walk your dog on a retractable leash, you may as well strap your dog into a vest of explosives, your dog is basically an armored weapon, and you're lucky if that leash doesn't end up wrapped around a telephone pole or a cyclist's wheel or your own fingers, which then need to be amputated. For years I told Nathan, Never get a retractable leash, and also, when meeting other dogs, don't be swayed by the cheap cuties, but he was too young to appreciate the difference between cuteness and physical appeal. Once we met a small, fluffy dog named Snowball whom Nathan mistook as the beau ideal. He showered the dog's head with sloppy kisses while I hung back, stiff with disbelief. The truth is Nathan adores all dogs; all he has to do is see a dog and his heart swings open like a barn door. It could be a scurfy, three-legged whippet with one eye and Nathan would want to go pet it. So naturally his heart swung wide open for the corgi in the park.

There's nothing wrong, I told him later, when we left in a rush, with the corgi in the park as compared to other corgis. It is corgis in general that are a problem—the dwarfish anatomical disaster that is breed standard.

The bat ears and the stubby legs, the huge head and the black-rimmed prostitute eyes; the length of the body, the absence of a tail! The breed is engineered to make people smile, specifically those people who need to patronize an animal in order to love it. But if you really love dogs, you don't want to see them humiliated and genetically maimed in the name of cuteness. People who own corgis tend to be frivolous people; they tend, in fact, to have a puerile habit of treating their dogs as substitute children. Hence the corgis who ride in backpacks and strollers, the corgis who wear clothes. If you Google "corgi"—which regrettably I've done—you'll find a cottage industry of cuteness: corgi calendars and corgi magnets, corgi shirts and corgi towels, corgi-lovers who don't even own corgis but waste their time swooning over corgis' achondroplastic heads and freakish butts. I saw a corgi in a banana costume, a corgi dressed up as a lobster! Corgis aren't dogs, they're just laughable cuddle toys with stubby legs and dopey eyes bred to entertain the bourgeois dregs of humanity, and this one seemed no exception, which is probably why Nathan fell all over it, feeding her the last of his croissant ("I bought that croissant for you, young man!") and asking the woman in the faux-fur bucket hat questions about the enfeebled, pop-eyed maniac who one minute was licking crumbs out of Nathan's hand and the next was nipping his ankles. That dog is a cartoon, not an animal, I wanted to say to Nathan, but there was no time to say anything at all because suddenly Walter lunged.

Moments later I was thinking: If only we hadn't stopped to talk to the corgi! If only Nathan hadn't fed the corgi; if only the corgi hadn't nipped; if only Walter hadn't lunged; if only I hadn't tripped on the retractable leash; if only the woman hadn't been screaming at the top of her lungs and Walter had been able to hear my commands . . . but you could fill a grocery cart with if's and, at the end of the day, still have nothing to eat.

The corgi died. Walter snapped her neck like she was a rabbit.

PART TWO

Chapter 1

The most comforting dessert I know is a chocolate cream pie. I got this recipe from a woman in an elevator when I was totally new to dairy-free cooking. We were on the eighth floor of the Rotary building, I was coming down from the dentist, I don't even remember how this stranger and I got to talking, but by the time we hit the lobby, I knew to throw twelve ounces of silken tofu and twelve ounces of melted chocolate chips into the blender. Dump in a pie shell, chill, and serve. Sometimes I add chocolate almond milk or half a cup of almond butter. But you don't have to. Just three ingredients make an amazing pie, and I swear, nobody *ever* knows they're eating tofu.

Or you can just make the chocolate filling and eat it out of a jar.

We didn't linger at the park. Panicked, I thought only of getting Walter out before the other lady got crazy and demanded vengeance. I muttered a few broken sentences, I'm sure, as I leashed up Walter, and then we hotfooted it down the block. But the fantasy of a clean escape quickly acquired some dinge. A block from home I realized a white van marked ANIMAL PATROL was rolling three feet behind us.

The van stopped and a woman emerged in full police uniform. She had questions for me. Who wouldn't?

Has your dog ever bitten a dog before? (No.) Has he ever bitten you or any other person? (No.) Is he up to date on his rabies? (Yes.) Do you think the other woman is a lunatic? (Yes. The dog warden didn't ask the last one, I only wish she had.) All through the interview Nathan danced up and down, singing nonsense and clapping his hands, sometimes patting his belly, or skipping. When he erupted in a shout of laughter, I burst into tears, and the dog warden assumed I was crying because of the corgi. Which I was, but also I was crying because Nathan was acting like I'd taken him to Cirque du Soleil. Meanwhile Walter wagged his tail and jostled the warden as if he expected an open palm of Milk-Bones. The cognitive dissonance was overwhelming. I cried for an embarrassingly long time. I was still crying when the warden explained she didn't deem Walter dangerous.

In Evanston, a dangerous dog isn't defined as a dog who kills a dog, or even as a dog who bites a person, but as a dog who bites a person *three* times. So Walter, thank goodness, would not be impounded.

A squirrel flashed across the elm above, releasing a sparkling explosion of snow. Walter barked madly.

Of course, the dog warden went on, the corgi owner could come after me in civil court for property damages. She gave me the owner's info and advised me to make amends.

At home I threw myself into making a chocolate cream pie. As I was rattling around the kitchen, I called Omar, who said, Leave Walter at home and come on over to the shop. Once I finish up here, I said as Nathan bounced in to lick the spatula.

"Aunt Rose, at the park, did you see her jump into me?"

He meant the corgi. Normally I would have said, You mean jump *on* me, not *into* me; but I was in no mood to correct his grammar. I'd seen the corgi nip his ankles before Walter—you know. I asked, Was Nathan scared of Walter now?

Walter lay at my feet, his nose on his paws. When I said his name, he looked up.

"Silly old Walter, no!" Nathan planted a kiss on his large-domed head.

Walter thumped his tail.

It had been a moment, I decided. Why punish a dog or treat him like a felon? I didn't want to muzzle Walter. Whenever I see a muzzled dog on the sidewalk, I swerve away and think *Cujo*. I thought: I'll just be careful about where I walk him, how close I let him get to other dogs, especially smaller dogs, neurotic dogs, food-centered dogs, and dogs with crazy owners and retractable leashes.

"Want to hear one of her knock-knock jokes?" Nathan
said.

"Whose?"

"Hazel. The dog from the park."

"You made up her name?"

"She told me her name when she came over."

"Who came over?"

"Hazel. Her soul. So merry and so gamesome! She's
dead and not dead! Can I open another bag of chocolate
chips?"

"You can open anything in the cupboard," I said,
and we left it at that.

An hour later, I drove to the Dive Shop, the chocolate
cream pie in the back seat, next to a jumble of dog treats,
wet wipes, and poop bags.

"Knock knock."

"Who's there?"

"Hazel."

"Hazel who?"

"Hazel cloud your view of reality!"

I didn't laugh. "Hey! Don't stick your head out the
car window. If you sit in the front seat, you need to sit
like a normal person."

"We're just smelling!"

Who's *we*? I might have thought, but just then pro-
nouns were beyond me. By the time Nathan rolled up
the window and settled into his seat, I crackled with

irritation. As he fumbled with his seatbelt, I switched on the radio. In a slow, calm baritone the announcer said, "A tone poem by Richard Strauss. Till Eulenspiegel's Merry Pranks, Opus 28 . . ."

"Let's not talk," I said. "Let's just listen."

Chapter 2

Frogman Dive Shop occupies a small storefront in a strip mall in Skokie. The window display is lousy—a bunch of old mannequins in dusty scuba gear—but people come in already knowing who Omar is. For years, before the accident, he certified people at the lakefront and sponsored dive trips to Mexico. Now he mostly sells equipment.

Omar gave Nathan snorkel masks to play with, and the two of us huddled in the back office, among boxes and curling posters of Belize. I was ready to settle with the corgi owner, I said, but scared she was already posting about Walter on Facebook, or papering the neighborhood with flyers.

"That's what *you* would do if someone killed Walter. Is this woman on social media?"

"I don't know anything about her, except she has bad taste in hats. Here's her name." I produced the dog warden's piece of paper.

"I liked her hat," Nathan called from the front of the shop. "And her soul. Omar, can I have a granola bar?"

"You can have three."

"Suddenly he's interested in souls," I muttered.

Omar opened his laptop and Googled Mary Munn, but didn't find anything. Not even LinkedIn. Lucky for me, I'd killed the dog of an internet nonentity. As we were celebrating this tiny win, the dive shop phone rang, but it was only the Dolphin Project calling to ask for money, so Omar let it go to voicemail and asked, How was Nathan? Had he cried yet?

Omar is big on crying; he keeps a playlist on his phone to induce tears and updates it piously. No, I'd already cried enough for both of us, I explained. Nathan was dry-eyed and cheerful. He capers, he giggles, he tells knock-knock jokes which the dead dog told him.

Eyes wide, Omar opened the door a crack. Nathan, snorkel masks dangling from his wrists like bracelets, babbled to the wall-hung fiberglass Queen Triggerfish.

"What else did he say?" Omar whispered.

What's a soul? Aunt Rose, can you see my soul?

"He prattles. I don't know. He pretends he's talking to the corgi."

Nathan shucked off the masks and wandered over to a wetsuit, whose sleeve he gently sucked.

"An imaginary friend is a coping strategy, Rose."

"And what's wrong with coping? I just wish he'd picked an imaginary person."

"No, no, no." Omar is ten years younger than I am and thinks every difficult experience is a trauma. "I think he's messed up from witnessing the dogfight."

"Come on, this isn't the same as witnessing a diver get the bends."

"She had a subarachnoid hemorrhage, and we're not talking about that."

"He knew the dog five minutes. I agree he's acting loopy—"

"Pretending the dog is alive? Total cry for help. I saw something about this on *Oprah*."

I hated this discussion, as I hated the misty, reverential look on Omar's face whenever he mentioned Oprah.

"What do you want me to do?"

"Understand he's grieving. Sit down and have a heart-to-heart."

"About what?"

"Death, sadness, the big stuff."

"I don't do heart-to-hearts. I'm more of a spleen-to-spleen person."

Which is true, though I try to make up for this with the occasional exquisite gesture. Speaking of which, I cheated a little with the chocolate cream pie recipe. I said three ingredients, and the third was a pie shell. You can buy a pre-made one, but since a dog was dead, I made my best vegan pie crust, which is: one cup of cashews, one cup of almonds, two-thirds cup of walnuts, a teaspoon of vanilla extract, and one and a third cups of pitted Medjool dates. Pulse in a food processor, press into a pie dish, and chill. Apologies (oh, so many apologies!) if you're allergic to nuts.

Chapter 3

The woman in the faux-fur bucket hat, aka Mary Munn, lived not far from the park in a mustard-yellow wood-frame house that had been divided into apartments. The sagging porch was littered with wrinkled circulars, advertisements no one read; snowed upon, dried, and snowed upon again. As we climbed the stairs, the sight of a tennis ball in the corner brought a lump to my throat. There were three mailboxes, three bells, three reasons not to go through with it, but I rang.

Mary opened the door: hatless, thirty-five or so, face blotchy from crying. "Huh!" she said and walked back into the house. She left her apartment door open—which I took as an invitation.

"Bad time?" My eyes adjusted to the dim of her disheveled living room. "I mean, obviously it's a bad time. Chocolate cream pie?"

"Pie?" she echoed.

"Yes, for you." As I waited for her to speak or extend her hands, I introduced Nathan. "My nephew," I said irrelevantly. "Age six. Staying with me a whole week!" Finally, receiving neither motion nor signal, I deposited the dish on a rickety side table on which lay a pile of unopened mail, a pair of fuzzy gloves, and a family-size bag of Sour Patch Kids. Mary blinked as if I'd performed a magic trick.

"You're a cook, huh?" she said after a queasy pause. "Kim always nags me about my kitchen skills. Kim, who boils ramen! But that's what abusers do, right? They twist all kinds of shit. Make you doubt yourself. Luckily I don't live in *her* shadow anymore."

Mary sat on a large, begrimed recliner and talked on, until we sank obediently onto the sofa opposite. Was she deranged with grief, or just deranged? It was easy to imagine how upset *I'd* be if Walter had been hastily dispatched in a public park. Why *did* Walter lash out? Was it the croissant? Or the corgi coming between him and Nathan? Resource-guarding, it's called when dogs fight over a toy. Jealousy, if we're talking about humans. I had time to think because Mary, blinking back tears, was rambling on about Kim. She seemed to have forgotten the dogs entirely. Then Nathan found and applied himself to a basket of squeaky toys, and she lit up like a kid who hears the ice cream van.

"Kim bought those! She never bought me a single birthday present, but look at all *that* stuff! Oh my god," Mary broke into a wheezy laugh, "remember the ballerina outfit? When Trevor took photos of her on the bathroom

58

floor with ketchup? It looked like *Black Swan*, right?" Her eyes filled with tears. "He got a million likes."

Nathan found and held the dog dress up for our admiration, a humiliation of satin and mesh.

I coughed. "Mary, maybe I should have called first. We've sort of barged in here and taken you by surprise. Do you know who I am?"

"The people from the park," she rasped. Her eyes seemed to go in and out of focus. Slowly and awkwardly I apologized, explaining I'd come to recompense her, even though money couldn't possibly make up for the loss. When I produced a check, Mary took it like I'd handed her a tapeworm. She shook her head and closed one eye, either to express skepticism or because she had an eyelash stuck. Honestly, I found her hard to read.

I explained how I arrived at the number.

"I looked up the current market value of a Pembroke Welsh corgi, to be purchased from a reputable American Kennel Club breeder. Then I factored in basic obedience and a few supplies. When trying to estimate funeral expenses, I didn't know whether you'd choose cremation or burial, so I tried to be generous and calculated cremation by the pound. I apologize if this all seems crass," I added when her head nodded forward. She appeared to be drowsing. "I, of all people, understand what a dog means—as a friend, a companion—but at the same time, I think we should remember, just so we don't end up in some ridiculously protracted and petty negotiation, that no amount of money can bring your corgi back to you."

"She wasn't a corgi," Mary murmured, studying a spider on the ceiling.

"In exchange—I mean, should you accept this small but generously intended compensation, I ask only that you agree not to talk about Walter on social media, or in public, or to any of your friends."

Mary exploded into a great, hacking cough. "Who's Walter?"

I cleared that up in two seconds, after which Mary explained the corgi didn't belong to her. "See, when Kim went to live with Patty on a wind farm in Wisconsin, she left me with the rent, the cable bill, and the dog. I know it sucks to talk shit about the dead—"

"She's dead and not dead," Nathan said.

"—but last month she ate a pack of sponges, a bike seat, and a container of my landlord's tile sealer. He threatened to evict me if I couldn't stop her barking! And Rose? I can call you Rose, right? She wasn't a corgi. She was, I don't know, maybe a corgi-Chihuahua mix? Future-wise, you might want to get a better hold on your dog. He was kinda like a big black bat sprung from hell. Maybe a retractable leash. So you can reel him in?"

A squeaky toy replied. Nathan, rolling fervently on his back, was mouthing a plastic hamburger.

"But I couldn't dredge up anybody to take that dog. Anita gave her back after two days, Bobby Umali after two hours. Do you know Bobby Umali? He fixes bikes. Anyway Kim knew. From day one, I told her I'm a cat person, then one night she and Lenny drop acid and decide it's hilarious to buy a mutt on Craigslist. Red flag, am I right? Take your dog with you to the wind farm! But water under the bridge, okay?"

"What do you mean?" I said, unable to follow her disordered mind.

"I mean it's no biggie." And with this dignified clarification, Mary tore up my check.

Chapter 4

Obviously Mary Munn was batshit. Why didn't she take my check? Nathan didn't care about the economic consequences, but he noticed the tenor of Mary's remarks, and on the ride home he said, "She didn't love Hazel? She didn't love her dog at all?" Love makes people brainsick, I explained. The corgi was her girlfriend's dog, so Mary's glad to be rid of it. To demonstrate my open-mindedness, I said, "If she doesn't want the check, I can't make her take it," mentally adding: What an idiot!

That was Sunday. Not at all the Sunday I had planned. At home I buried my face in Walter's fur, and Nathan sat beside me, squeezing a squeaky donut—Mary Munn had gifted him the toy basket. Then he flipped through my binder and found the meal plan.

"Sunday says Sweet N Spicy Bean Cakes with Cashew Cream Dressing. Kale, Apple, and Walnut Salad." Getting no answer, he flipped to the design section. "Hey, that's the exact same lamp that's in my room. And there's the bed and nightstand. And the rocking chair. Are these

numbers price tags? I like these paint colors. Glowstick
Yellow. Barton-upon-Humber Blue. Aunt Rose, I can
eat the saltwater taffy, right? In the fancy jar? Or is that
decoration?"

He inched over to where I lay on the floor and ran
his hands through Walter's fur. Then he stretched one
arm under the Louis XV sofa and grasped blindly for a
tennis ball. He threw it down the hallway, but Walter
wanted to sleep.

"Well," Nathan said earnestly. "Are you going to
get up and make the Sweet N Spicy Bean Cakes soon?"

"I'm just feeling a little bit tired."

"Grown-ups are always tired." After a pause, he gal-
loped off to the Wevet room, where he took a decorative
tennis racket off the wall. I closed my eyes and listened to
it whistle as he swung it through the air. Then he fetched
Walter's ball and smashed it around, probably denting the
new paint job. I didn't care, even though I'd hired the
Michelangelo of house painters. I woke up to Nathan
standing over me, panting and frowning.

"When Mommy gets tired, we eat scrambled eggs
for dinner."

"I don't have eggs. I think the chicken industry is
the most abusive—"

"Do you have peanut butter?"

I did and it was a great idea. We ate it on crackers
while Nathan told knock-knock jokes, to which I listlessly
responded. Then he sidled off and took a shower. When

he emerged, wet-haired and pajama-clad, I said, "Pick a number, any number."

"Two," he said, and we sat on the sofa and listened to Mahler 2.

"I wonder what Mommy and Daddy are doing now," he said as the furious funeral march began to play. Drinking, I thought with bitter hopefulness. Brewing the argument that will explode before the vacation's end. Nathan hoped they were swimming with dolphins. I told him I hoped not, tourism shouldn't exploit wildlife, I'd sent his parents links to the Humane Society and the Dolphin Project.

"Hey, Aunt Rose, want to hear what I can do? I just learned it."

He sat up on his haunches and barked—a long, hysterical volley of high-pitched barks.

"Wow! But can you do this?" I gave him my Common Loon, several fruity hoots that rise to an eerie, wavering alarm and climax with a strangled yodel (Danger on the Lake: A Tragicomedy in Three Acts). He'd never heard me do it—or frankly, anything like it.

"Is there a loon inside of you?"

"No," I said. "It's just an impression I used to do for fun."

I sang another undulating tone, and he scrabbled around on the sofa, barking, and tossing my throw pillows like they were dice.

"Listen," I said later when he was tucked in under the poppy-bright bedspread. "I was a little off my head today, and I want to be sure you're not traumatized or anything."

"Nope."

"I didn't think so, but Omar asked me to check. Tomorrow I'll make a good dinner, and after you do your homework, we'll play a proper game of chess. I wish we'd never stopped to pet that corgi, but life rolls on, right?"

"You can say that again! It rolls on and on and on. Aunt Rose, I'm glad we stopped to pet Hazel! Hazel says—"

"I'm not interested in what Hazel says. Death is sad but final, Nathan. Like when a junky toy from Target breaks and you throw it away. Let's stop pretending that dog is still around."

He closed his eyes. "I'm not pretending. She's in me."

"In you where?"

"Inside and all over." He touched his belly and his head; he lay his hand on his heart. "She kind of moves around. And she talks a lot. I tried to tell you before. When her body died, Hazel wasn't sure where she was supposed to go. Or what she was supposed to do. So she leaped into me. Never mind! Hazel said you wouldn't believe me. She said you're limited by your senses."

"*I'm* limited?"

"Not just you, lots of people. Hold on, she says she'll come out."

65

Then he closed his eyes, and though every window in the Wevet room was closed, a cold wind billowed the custom-made drapes, rattled the decorative tennis rackets, and flooded the air with the meaty smell of biscuits. An electric feeling crept from the top of my scalp to the base of my spine, and my mouth filled with something sweet and salty and, texturally, revolting. What kind of trick was this? But my teeth chattered too much to speak. The poppy-bright comforter blew up off the bed, and in a panic I reached for him, but recoiled because my hands touched fur. The wind died down and there she lay, in his place, the corgi from the park—that stupid little dog, with stubby legs and bat ears, huge head and black-rimmed prostitute eyes, beaming. She wagged her tailless rump, cocked her head, and my beloved nephew's high, bubbly giggle spurted out of her mouth.

Chapter 5

I've always thought of my bedroom as the perfect sanctuary. Cream-colored walls, botanical prints, Spanish colonial queen—serpentine pilasters, turned bun feet. Usually, I walk in and feel a deep, abiding calm, the way I felt as a child when the teacher properly cleaned the blackboards. But after the corgi, I was afraid to go to my room. Afraid to go to bed. I turned on every light in the house and sat on the Louis XV sofa, encased in thick, cold fear.

Eventually I fetched a bottle of whisky and texted Omar. "Something weird just happened," I said, and in retrospect, that's called burying the lede. Out to dinner, he texted back. He'd catch me later.

Fuck.

You don't realize how small your life has become until something wreaks havoc, until the pin is removed on which the threads of reality hang. I had friends besides Omar, but suddenly they seemed more like friend-proxies: people I socialized with in the dairy industry, acquaintances with whom I occasionally had coffee or lunch, a college friend who married a lantern-jawed Libertarian, upon which we drifted, somewhat bitterly, apart. None of them seemed remotely appropriate to call up at nine o'clock on a Sunday night and say, "I think my nephew is possessed by a corgi."

Should I call Victor and Astrid? How would I even lay it out to them? *Walter killed a corgi, and the corgi's soul jumped into Nathan's body. You see, the corgi was unpleasant in life and now she's dead, she's still making trouble. I don't know where dead dogs are supposed to go, but apparently this one is way off course.* No, it was crazy. Out of the question. What could they do about it anyway from Mexico?

The corgi had remained for ten seconds—maybe less—and then Nathan lay in bed alone again, a film of sweat on his brow. His deep breathing had the rhythm of sleep. I drank too much whisky, scrolled through my contacts, and dialed my high school friend Deb, who lives in Houston.

Ten years ago Deb married a wealthy finance guy and was enslaved to her teenage step-kids, slobby asshole football players for whom she spent her days doing thankless errands. When the boys weren't home, she worried they were off raping junior high school girls. She answered on the first ring, and I asked right away if she was busy. No, she was watching Netflix and eating jelly beans.

"Did you ever see the viral video *Corgi Pool Party?*" she said when I told her what I'd witnessed. "Six corgis jumping into the deep end, sliding down a water slide. You even see their stubby legs paddling underwater. Adorable!"

"Did you hear what I said?"

"You think you saw a ghost. Let's back up. Did Walter bark?"

"He wasn't in the room."

"Did the bed spin?"

"No, but the comforter—"

"Did any windows fly open—any drawers?"

"I don't think so, but it got cold, and the drapes blew around."

"Solid corgi or flickering?"

"Solid. Well, maybe it flickered a little. Solid *and* flickering."

"You'd think it would be either/or."

Deb noisily ate a handful of jelly beans.

"Maybe you saw a ghost. But I don't know. Maybe you just feel bad about Walter's accident and imagined you did."

"I can't believe you're doubting me. You were Wiccan in high school."

"I was depressed in high school."

"You're still more metaphysical than I am. You did ninth-grade Astrology Club."

"With that creepy Mr. Garr, who helped us draw our birth charts. Then he sent Tiffany Uggam on an errand, got me alone, and said I was more mature than other girls because I had Saturn in my first house." She began to cry softly. "My god, I don't want to remember this."

"I'm sorry, Deb."

I hated Mr. Garr, I still think he should be in prison. Instead he became a TV producer and won an Emmy for a six-part documentary about the endangered Black Rhino.

"Deb, what would you do if you had an unwanted spirit in one of your kids?"

"If it was in Mike or Thad? I'd kill him. I'd love the excuse. But then—maybe then it would come into me." She paused. "This is too heavy, Rose."

She lit a joint and we talked about other things. I gave her my six-ingredient recipe for vegan crackers, and we speculated whether or not she could substitute weed for the Italian seasoning. By the time we got off the phone, it was late and Walter had slunk out of the living room. Sad and solitary, I broke my personal rules about not texting someone after ten, and not texting someone when they haven't texted me back, and texted Omar. It took about fourteen texts to explain. He sent back an *Exorcist* GIF, the one where Linda Blair does the spider walk.

"This is no joke," I typed.

Three little dots appeared, and then faded. Curled like a shrimp on my straight-backed sofa, I drifted to sleep.

Chapter 6

In the morning I woke with a dead phone and a sharp, shooting pain from neck to sacrum. My head ached, my mouth tasted like I'd been chewing compost. Had I imagined the whole thing? I recycled the whisky bottle and wove through the house, switching off lights. Walter was asleep on my bed, sprawled like a king. Nathan's door was closed. Phone charged, I checked for messages. Nothing from Omar, but around four a.m. Deb had sent a screenshot.

Seeking help, attached entity! the internet post began. An EMT was working the defibrillator when his patient died. Suddenly the EMT developed a taste for tequila and was drawn to gambling and porno sites, all of which he attributed to the dead man's spirit. **He couldn't have gotten in unless I have cracks in my aura, but how do I seal up the cracks???**

Below this post, several people with nutjob usernames offered prayers as well as their services as long-distance healers.

I read the post three times before Deb called.

"Cracks in the aura? Attached entity? It's Monday, Deb. I have to function."

"Functioning's overrated. Want the link? Hold on, Thad's screaming— Not in the *pantry* . . . I don't know, wherever the hell *you* put it— See, after we hung up, I read all this shit about ghost dogs. But usually a ghost is a wispy image, or a creaking floorboard, or a brush against your legs. And you said she's *inside* him, right? So I broadened my search terms. And that's when I hit the mother lode."

I winced at the expression. Not everyone's mother is a rich gold vein, let alone a source of desirable qualities. But who had time to quibble?

"Unload the lode," I said.

"Soul possession." Deb paused to let the phrase seep in. "Dark entities attaching to your soul and choking you like a weed."

"Dog entities?"

"Dark entities, living in your body like a parasite, feeding off your energies and pulling your strings."

"Are you still high?"

"Cannabis stays in your system for forty minutes."

"Oh my god."

"You should've experimented more in high school, Rose."

In high school my father was dead and my mother was dying.

"Did you read anything about dogs?" I asked. "Anyone specifically taken over by a dog soul?"

"No."

"Why is this happening to me?" I wailed.

"Technically, it's not happening to you. It's happening to him."

This was an excellent point. "But he's too pleased for it to be a dark entity," I pointed out. "Nathan's excited when he talks to her, like he's doing show-and-tell."

"You need to educate yourself about occult phenomena. Get online," Deb commanded, but that was out of the question. Chat rooms, social media platforms, electronic bulletin boards—people routinely misunderstand my tone. I used to post on a midcentury pottery and glass forum, but the so-called community kept flagging my posts. Now I confine myself to Tripadvisor and Yelp, and even there a person is vulnerable to random censure. (When Yelp removed my review of The Grüne Tavern, I felt the same level of anguish I did when a band of teenagers egged my house.) Seriously, I thought I'd crack up if I started reading stuff online.

Instead I opened a package of rice paper and whisked together a marinade: four tablespoons of nutritional yeast, a tablespoon of garlic powder, six tablespoons of soy sauce, one tablespoon of maple syrup, a teaspoon of smoked paprika, half a teaspoon of liquid smoke. If you dip the rice paper in this sauce and bake it for seven minutes, you have vegan bacon, which means none of the saturated fat or chemical additives that cause cancer. Aunt Edith, the one who took the paint-by-numbers oil of a weeping clown off the wall so Victor and I could sleep without nightmares, died of colorectal cancer. Which is tragic, even though she, like my mother, took no joy in life.

"Does it sound to you like one of those dark entities?" I asked Deb as I sliced rice paper into strips. The oven was already preheating. (Four hundred.)

"Was the corgi confrontational?"

"It laughed."

"At you or with you?"

"I don't know!"

"I guess you'll know soon if it *is* a dark entity. People start breaking shit. And masturbating inappropriately. And cursing like sailors. And hurting other people—well, I mean, whatever. It'll be clear."

Chapter 7

It might strike you as odd, or hypocritical, or maybe just embarrassing, but my plan for Monday's breakfast was to make pancakes. In my defense, Nathan likes them, and I'd researched egg replacements.

In fact, I'd over-researched them. Aquafaba or apple-sauce? Mashed banana or flaxseed? Baking soda or arrow-root? Ghost dog or dark entity? Obviously I was delaying the moment I had to wake Nathan and confront my fears. Because what if I opened the door to the Wevet room and found the corgi panting in his place? What if she'd trashed the room? Or what if she'd killed him in the night? I stopped dithering, dropped my spoon, and raced down the hall. There he lay, starfished on the top sheet, the comforter puddled on the floor, his plush rabbit, Whippy, pinned under one arm.

He'd had a good night. He'd dreamed he was a puppy. In a litter box . . . with all these other puppies . . . warm, cold, hungry, thirsty . . . running in a muddy field . . .

He didn't appear moody, let alone murderous.

In the kitchen, we made the batter together. (Aquafaba is a cheap and miraculous egg replacer. You just add a little sugar to the chickpea water and use a stand mixer to produce a thick and creamy foam.) While I drank coffee and nibbled a sheet of nori, Nathan crowed, with satisfaction, about recent events. Unlike me, he had no sense of a crisis.

"Remember how Mommy said dogs are too much work? And when I said, Can we get a cat? she said, I'm not a cat person, and when I said, How about a guinea pig, she said no, they smell. Remember, Aunt Rose? I said, How about a hamster? How about a grasshopper mouse?"

I flipped the pancakes. "I remember."

"Remember I said, How about a python? and she said snakes are nasty. And I kept asking. Mommy, I want any pet. I'd be happy with a ferret, or a turtle, or a Pac-man Frog! I said, Daddy, didn't you have tetras when you were a kid? I even begged for a fish tank, but all I got for Christmas was a bunch of LEGOs and clothes and a stupid glockenspiel."

I served the pancakes. "That glockenspiel was from—"

"But now I have a dog!" He smiled broadly. "A real dog. Just like you, Aunt Rose. Except," he added thoughtfully, "she's inside."

"I'm wondering what we're going to do about that."

"Why do anything?" he asked and began to eat the pancakes with his hands. His eyes were bright, his cheeks enflamed, his hair appeared to have grown in six new directions overnight.

"Slow down. Use a fork."

"I like Hazel!"

"Nathan, don't lap the plate."

"I had a granola bar for lunch and crackers for dinner. Me and Hazel are hungry!"

He raised his sticky chin and threw me a pitiful look, like Oliver Twist in the workhouse. *Hazel and I*, I thought, but the correction stifled under pangs of remorse. Regular meals. Homework. Bedtime. A ride to and from school. What else had I promised? Now I needed to pack his lunch. Wait, he had a corgi inside him! Should he go to school?

"Why wouldn't I?" he said. "I don't have a fever."

I checked; he didn't have a fever. "Okay, we'll proceed as planned, but don't mention 'Hazel' to Ms. Shingler, or Tommy, or anyone."

"Because she's a dog?" he asked as I slathered hummus into a pita.

"Because she's a ghost. Or an entity. Whatever she is."

"She's just a soul, Aunt Rose. And I think she's fun."

"Jesus Christ." I threw some baby carrots and bacon into a compostable bag and glanced at the oven clock. "What time's the first bell?"

"Five minutes ago."

I swatted him out of his chair.

Chapter 8

Rawlings Elementary School is a long, low building, built in the 1960s, its brick walls punctuated with small, narrow windows, as if someone thought children wouldn't learn if they could look out. For years I told Victor and Astrid I'd pay for private school, and now I was reminded why. On the playground a clutch of boys played keep-away with a red snow boot; against a brick wall girls lined up as if they expected to be shot; alone and unobserved, some boy did a jig as he twisted all the swing set chains. What a hellhole!

Nathan popped open the passenger door.

"Clear on the plan?" I said.

"Don't mention Hazel."

I made him pinky-promise and high-five before he went off.

The boy at the swing set quit the jig and whipped off his earmuffs. Then I recognized him: Tommy Bessinger. Who even wears earmuffs anymore? Weirdo!

Waiting for the traffic to clear, I texted Omar the screenshot.

"Where did you get this?" he asked when he called five minutes later.

"Deb sent it."

"Deb who worshiped the Great Horned God in high school? The one who stabbed voodoo dolls of her teacher?"

"He molested her. I don't have time to look for reputable paranormal studies."

"Why don't you check out a parenting website, or *Psychology Today*?"

"You should've been with me when it happened, Omar."

"I was at the symphony, remember?" he said quickly.

"I just wish you'd seen Nathan wolfing down pancakes this morning. He was eating like a dog. Last night he was barking."

But according to Omar, creative play was a coping device. I must be suffering from a temporary delusion. "I believe *you* believe you" was how he put it, even after I explained I'd smelled biscuits and felt the corgi's fur. I elaborated on what I'd texted: The meat I'd tasted in my mouth was prosciutto, and prosciutto was heart attack food.

"So the thing knows I'm Jewish! It knows I'm vegetarian! Obviously it's fucking with me!"

Omar sighed. "Maybe it's time to give the moral judgments about food a rest. This is what's driving you crazy in your work life. You're so harsh about what everybody eats. If you could ever forgive yourself for launching a dairy business—"

"But prosciutto—"

"Turn off the car, Rose. Are you still driving?"

I pulled over and cut the engine.

"Maybe it was too much—agreeing to look after Nathan for a week. Especially with the Cultured Cow deal falling apart. You haven't had time to process that, and then this thing with Walter. Were you drinking last night?"

"It's a thing, Omar—spiritual parasites! They attach themselves to a living host and drain their energy. They make a person do crazy stuff."

"Such as?"

"Masturbate, Deb says. But worse—drugs. Alcohol. And violence."

"Masturbate?" He laughed. "I love you, Rose, but stop reading sketchy chat rooms. Take a deep breath. You have to be the adult here. That's what you wanted, right? To take care of Nathan? So just because you feel guilty about that dead corgi, don't get carried away. Honestly, you might need therapy to process your feelings about Walter's aggression—but not this week. This week is about taking care of Nathan. Right?"

"Right," I said, but only because I knew he didn't believe me.

"And by the way, not every therapist is like your father."

Omar never even met my parents. A few moss-covered anecdotes and he thought he had a PhD on my childhood.

"Bye, Omar," I said and hung up.

Chapter 9

At Cultured Cow, I told Pearl to hold all calls and hung the DO NOT DISTURB sign on my door. Then I pulled the shades and sprawled on the industrial carpet. I don't know why, but it seemed impossible to sit upright in a chair. On top of my shock that Nathan was possessed by a corgi, I was shocked by how easily I'd adjusted to the fact that Nathan was possessed by a corgi. I always thought people who believed in ghosts were stupid or frightened or morbid. Even though we read ghost stories in school, I never considered they might be real. That shade who begs Odysseus to bury him? Metaphor for unfinished business. Hamlet's father? Creaky plot device. The afterlife? A Christian concept as relevant as the Easter Bunny. Although maybe Jewish people did believe in souls; I didn't know, having received less than an ounce of religious instruction. At Share Your Heritage Day, I'd talked more about bagels than the Bible. Where did Jewish people think souls fluttered off to? I was in spiritual kindergarten, and who was I going to ask?

"Knock knock." Doug D'Andrea pushed open the office door and blushed.

"Kink in my back," I explained as I lumbered off the floor. "Slept on the Louis XV."

"We have a little problem, Rose. The European market in Glencoe reported packaging bloat. Not every flavor, but fourteen cases of Gotcha Matcha."

"*Mucor circinelloides.*" I smoothed my clothes.

"Maybe. We need to test."

"What a bummer! Well, process the returns . . ."

"Obviously. And investigate the supply chain."

I nodded absently. "*Mucor* isn't a disease-causing food-borne pathogen."

"We don't know yet if it is *Mucor*. Maybe"—he winced, hand on chest—"we should think about a voluntary recall."

"Is that your acid reflux?"

"It's stress-related."

"It's dairy-related. Cut the milk from your coffee and you'll see. Listen, Doug, I just saw a ghost."

"I just saw a zombie in the parking lot. About the returns—"

"I'm serious. And I hadn't been drinking. I drank after."

"I'm losing the thread."

"What if you saw a ghost? What would be your first thought?"

"Toxic mold."

"Why?"

"A lot of paranormal experiences turn out to be hallucinations caused by fungal spores."

"That's fascinating."

"Is it?" he said doubtfully.

"Yes! Dogs are susceptible to respiratory diseases, so for Walter's sake I keep the moisture levels between thirty and fifty percent. I know I don't have mold." I beamed. "I'm glad you popped in, Doug. We haven't talked for a while."

"Let's look into electronic nose technology. If we had an e-nose, we could detect spoilage before we ship."

"I need a coffee! Want a coffee?"

"Goodness no," he said, hand on chest.

As Doug and I stood in line at Starbucks, I asked about his religious background, forgetting you're not supposed to ask employees that kind of thing.

"Unitarian," he said.

"Do Unitarians believe in ghosts?"

"Not really. Unitarians believe in the oneness of the whole of creation."

"You can ask for soy milk."

"I like it black."

"Suit yourself. I've never liked the word 'creation.' Aren't I the one creating my life? Let's grab that table. Why would I choose to believe we're all children bumbling around His playground until the great creator calls us home to sit on His lap?"

"You might be confusing God with Santa."

"The patriarchal shades, that's how people like me get thrown out of religion. Not that I was ever in. My parents didn't join a temple. They preferred Neil Diamond records and a weak friendship network. What was your husband raised? Same thing?"

"No, he's Jewish."

"John is?"

"Eric."

"I think I have a block when it comes to colleagues' personal lives. Is Eric Jewy Jewish or secular Jewish?"

"He likes to celebrate Hanukkah. While I have your ear, Gotcha Matcha! hasn't been moving well. I know you've got one foot out the door—"

That's when I realized I hadn't told Doug the deal fell through. He planned to stay at The Cow even after I sold it, but still—it was an oversight.

"Gotcha Matcha!" I said stupidly. "I eat it at my dacha!"

"All those months making the green-and-white swirl," Doug went on. "And when people eat it, they stir it into a uniform muck. And now with the packaging bloat—it's a bit of a fiasco. Let's call back the product, rather than just trace the batch."

"Too much media attention. Swab the factory and let's wait for the labs. We bought too much matcha to discontinue that flavor. Inclusions are just challenging."

"Could we discuss it at the staff meeting?"

"What staff meeting?"

He colored slightly. "I know you like to work alone. But I think it would be good for the team to reinstitute staff meetings."

"The team? It isn't baseball, Doug. We make artisanal yogurt."

"But morale." He lay a nail-bitten hand on his chest.

So—"The fungal subphylum *Mucor circinelloides* is used in natural flavor compounds," I explained an hour later to the nervous gang around the conference table, "and can easily cause container bloat. I want to assure you, *Mucor* doesn't hurt people unless they have a super compromised immune system. Doug is processing the returns and tracing the rest of the batch. We've ordered swabs, but I'm optimistic. I suspect a refrigeration issue, either at European Market or, worst-case scenario, one of the delivery trucks."

"Have you considered a voluntary recall?" Sylvia Klausner said.

"We don't have enough data to support that."

"Are we halting production on that flavor?" Bill Whitaker said.

"And draw the attention of the FDA?"

"What are we going to do if someone gets sick before the labs come back?" Becca Favorite said.

"We'll cross that bridge if we come to it. Any other questions?" I asked the stunned faces.

"Why do these donuts taste weird?"

"They're vegan!"

"I guess that went well," Doug said afterwards, squeezing a purple stress ball.

"Like a holiday party, right? Only focused. By the way, Doug, the buyout is off. His financing fell through."

"What? When?"

I consolidated the uneaten donuts into a single bright pink box.

Chapter 10

"I ate three lunches today," Nathan told me after school. "The one you packed and half of Tommy's and all of Caitlynn's except her juice box. She wouldn't give me her juice box."

"Why are you swiping other people's lunches?"

"I didn't swipe! I was hungry and they gave 'em to me. Aunt Rose, didja ever think how funny it is that people sit at *desks*?"

I didn't think about it, not even when Nathan prompted, because I was busy thinking, That dark entity is a binge eater. Nathan banged on, picking his way through the donut box, explaining that Hazel found it hilarious to sit at a desk, and stand in line, and drink from a water fountain. Hazel found it amusing to eat with hands, and run on two legs, and open and close a door. To realize, as I was suddenly beginning to realize, that Hazel was working his body like a puppet was terrifying. She loved our light switches, Nathan reported. Today he was Light

Monitor. Next week he might be Pencil Monitor. And she only barked once—at the trash basket!

"Nobody knows about her. Honest. You can ask her."

I wasn't going to ask Hazel anything. I certainly suspected she'd have nothing nice to say. *Your dog killed me*, she might begin, and I'd say, I'd say—

"*Thou canst not say I did it.*" Nathan interrupted my thought. "*Never shake thy gory locks at me!* Oh, I forgot to tell you, Aunt Rose," he continued in a conversational tone, as if he hadn't heard the extraordinary words out of his own mouth, "when we went to the bathroom, Hazel said Rory Davis hasn't changed his underwear in three days, and Bubba, the janitor's son, is in jail for something he didn't even do, and Danny Bennett is going to get his appendix out, like an emergency, but he'll be fine, and then"—he exploded in giggles—"then I showed her how I aim my pee! But don't worry, nobody else was in the bathroom."

"Why's she telling you other people's private business? And where did you get those lines from Shakespeare?"

"What lines?"

He kept snarfing donuts. Overwhelmed, I grabbed a broom—had I heard that right?—and swept fur, crumbs, and sprinkles into a vile and tidy nest. Albert Einstein says the most important decision you make is whether you believe we live in a friendly or a hostile universe. I definitely believed in a hostile universe. I believed a dead thing was enticing Nathan with knock-knock jokes and trying to outwit me with allusions to *Macbeth*. As Nathan demolished the last chocolate brioche, I leaned on my broom.

"You can't let that dog use your mouth—or any other body parts! Stick up for yourself. You give the orders." I plucked the empty donut box from the table and crushed it into the recycling bin. "At the park that corgi saw you as an easy mark. And now she's inside, thinking she can get you to do whatever she wants. We need to let her know: You're in charge."

He didn't know what I meant, so I found a dog training video on YouTube. I don't know if this guy was an accredited trainer, but he had his own channel and said he could teach anyone to be a pack leader. He had a big, booming voice—like a cheese grater on my nerves—and looked like the sort of person I cross the street to avoid. "If you aren't the alpha," he warned, "you're the prey!" At first Nathan pranced around the room—"Zip-a-Dee-Doo-Dah! Does this mean I can keep her?"—but he sobered when he realized obedience was only my short-term strategy. We recited, I'm the alpha! I'm the alpha! half a dozen times, after which I wrote a reminder on a rainbow of Post-It notes and asked him to flag every surface in the house.

Dinner that night was lentil loaf, braised carrots, mashed potatoes, and greens. Don't worry, I'm not going to give you my recipe for lentil loaf. Truth be told, it was dry and underwhelming. But it was a comfort to be back on the meal plan I had meticulously designed, and more than food, I needed the satisfaction of completing tasks. Never before had I felt myself, morally, metaphysically, on such shaky ground.

During dinner, Walter hovered near the table, waiting for fork-falls. I talked fake-casually about the dangers of owning an ill-trained corgi who was given to the cheapest forms of wit. Nathan ate three helpings of everything and belched like a toad. Then he told more knock-knock jokes and laughed himself silly.

Pick a number, any number.

Six, Nathan said, and we listened to Mahler 6 as he gnawed a pencil and studied an idiotic worksheet on consonant blends.

"Your mom just texted to say you got a tardy slip this morning. I guess the school emailed her."

"Because we missed the first bell. But I have to get a hundred tardies before I get a detention, and then two hundred detentions before I get suspended. It's not a big deal. Tommy has thirty tardies."

"That school," I said with reflexive disdain. Most of the day the class sat at their desks doing worksheets, except for recess, when they were herded into the gym to watch *3 Ninjas*. Had he gone to the academy of my choice, one with a six-to-one student-teacher ratio, someone might have noticed Nathan was possessed by a corgi. Someone might have noticed him fondling doorknobs and barking at the trash basket. But tired Ms. Shingler hadn't noticed a thing.

"I like my school."

"And they like you. But do you always make your B's like that?"

"Like what?"

"Backwards." I tried to show him, but he didn't see what I meant.

"Maybe you write an old-fashioned way," he suggested.

"It's not old-fashioned, it's correct." His R's were back to front too. "You know that brochure I showed you, the one in the kitchen drawer? If you went to Alembic Academy, you could learn cursive."

"I like Rawlings, Tommy goes to Rawlings. His brothers go to Rawlings. Okay, I'm finished." He shoved the worksheet into his backpack so carelessly it would have more wrinkles tomorrow than W. H. Auden's face. "Now can we FaceTime?"

"No, if your parents hear what happened at the park, they might cancel their vacation and come home."

"To meet her?"

I made a noncommittal noise. After all the contempt they'd heaped on Walter, did he actually think his parents would be excited for him and his ghost dog? It confused me and made my chest feel hollow as an old stump.

Nathan sucked the collar of his T-shirt. "Well, what if we FaceTime them and don't mention Hazel?"

"Too risky. You're an open book. You tell them everything."

92

He spat out his collar. "I kept Hazel secret all day long."

"Yeah, but if your parents are there, asking you questions, you might slip up."

"Daddy says you're a nervous talker. Maybe you think *you'll* slip up."

"Your dad's a nervous eater. He's put on fifteen pounds since he married your mother."

Nathan's eyes grew wide. He bit his nails as Mahler 6 unfurled (lugubrious tuba, glacial flutes, raging brass).

"I didn't mean that," I told him.

"This is no fun."

"I said I didn't mean it. I just worry about your dad's weight."

"I wish I had an iPhone!"

"That's ridiculous. You're six."

"I'm six and three quarters."

"Well, it's silly. Nobody your age has a phone."

"Sofia Lopez has a phone. Keisha Washington has a phone."

"I don't know those kids."

"Tommy Bessinger has a phone."

"So he can fry his brain with games. I guess his parents don't read the studies on microwave radiation."

"Those studies use rats, not people. Mrs. Bessinger says—"

"I'm not going to argue it. Why does any six-year-old need a phone?"

"To call their parents!" he shouted.

Was I a terrible aunt? In the kitchen I went into overdrive—loading the dishwasher, scrubbing the stovetop grates, splashing the backsplash, removing clumps of Walter's fur from the baseboards.

"All right." I surged back into the living room. "We'll FaceTime them. But I'll make a list of what we can and can't talk about, and during the call, we'll keep the paper on the coffee table. If at any point you get confused, look down and check the list, all right?"

"Yes!" he yelled. "Hooray!"

In the left-hand column I wrote "OKAY" and listed whale sharks, chacalacas, homework, chess, what we ate for dinner, and Mahler. In the right-hand column I wrote "TOP SECRET" and kept it short: dogs, death, ghosts.

"My parents won't care about Mahler. Mommy likes Madonna and the Spice Girls. Daddy likes silence."

"Your father used to love Mahler." Was it possible he'd migrated that far since marriage? "Okay, I'm ready. Remember—if at any point you're not sure what to say, just look cute and let me do the talking."

He made a sardonic "cute" face. I gave Walter a carrot to chew in the other room and opened my laptop.

"Of course, your parents might not even be available right now," I warned.

They answered on the second ring.

Chapter 11

Sky, palm trees, swim deck. Dark strip of ocean.
   Victor and Astrid sat placidly on their hotel balcony,
margaritas in hand.

   The big news was they loved their resort. They had
barely said hello to the front desk when a man handed
them each a mimosa. They had barely unpacked their bags
when someone knocked on their door and offered them
fresh towels. They had barely stumbled into the elevator
when they realized the resort had ten restaurants, eight
bars, two dance clubs, and an infinity pool that spanned
a full city block and featured underwater speakers.

   "What about the beach?" Nathan asked.

   "No, not much beach. Turns out it's sargassum season. Disgusting algae bloom."

   "It's floating everywhere, and super smelly, like rot-
ten eggs. Can't swim."

   "Can you eat it? Aunt Rose eats seaweed for breakfast."

   "Does she? Ugh, no. We don't even touch it. There
might be jellyfish."

"Cool! What kind of jellyfish? Killer jellyfish?"

Victor and Astrid shrugged. Over and over he tried them—"Are they clear? Do they glow? Do they have crabs stuck on them? Are jellyfish older than dinosaurs? When was the first ever jellyfish?"—but they were curiously bad at answering his questions. Victor was advising him to wear water shoes any time he visited the beach when "Never mind!" Nathan interrupted, aware he'd sounded the depths of parental ignorance. "I'll ask Hazel."

"Ask who?"

"Nobody," I said. "Just a girl at school."

"Speaking of school!" Astrid chirped and began to explain Rawlings's bell system because she hoped I wouldn't let Nathan get another tardy. Victor went off to the minibar and got potato chips. Nathan's head listed to one side.

"Aunt Rose," he suddenly whispered, eyes dilated, cheeks pink, "Hazel says you can too eat sargassum."

"Ix-nay on azel-Hay," I whispered back, but he didn't know pig Latin. Left-hand column words only, I indicated with a finger jab.

"Oh, right. Then I choose the chess set," he announced plainly. "Aunt Rose says chess is better than checkers. Because it has more moves. But have you ever set up a chess board, Mommy? The black queen starts on a black square, Aunt Rose said, and *I* said, We have a blue queen, and a blue square, and we have a white queen and a white square, and *she* said, The rule in chess is you always say

96

black and white, even if your pieces are every color of the fucking rainbow."

There was a pause.

"How was the game?" Victor asked.

"I'm sure I didn't say the f-word."

"Actually," Nathan went on capably, "we didn't play. We went over the rules for another million hours. If you touch it, you move it. No skipping turns. The knight moves this way, and the rooks move that way, and the bishops move *another* way, and you can't just make them talk in squeaky voices, because you're out to capture prisoners and stuff."

"Everybody's ranked," I explained.

"Maybe chess isn't his speed," Astrid said.

"Maybe not," Nathan said, and instantaneously brightened. "Knock knock!" he shouted.

"Who's there?" his parents said in unison.

"Hazel." He opened his eyes and crossed them, and just as his parents chanted, "Hazel who?" his cheeks rippled and his nose elongated—and for an instant, there was *her* muzzle! In a gust of panic I whacked the display so the camera faced the coffee table. Then I hung up.

"What the hell was *that*?" I asked Nathan, my joints looser than jelly.

Muzzle gone, he shook with laughter. "Hazel says it's FACETime! Get it? Get it?"

Fear had me by the throat.

"Remember the agreement? No dogs. No peekaboo."

"You didn't say no jokes!"

"But you knew I meant no Hazel. Be the alpha, Nathan. Make her lie low."

"That's no fun. She's never talked to Mommy and Daddy."

As we argued, my laptop began to ring, but I refused to pick up until he *promised*.

"Did anything look strange just now?" I asked them.

No. It was a miracle. They'd missed the muzzle.

Low resolution pic?

Drunk and inattentive?

Abruptly Nathan announced he was *bored with my rules* and ran off to the kitchen to find Walter.

"He sounds a little cranky," Victor said. "Everything all right there?"

"Everything's great."

"You can tell us if he's giving you trouble."

"He's never trouble. Chess is more fun than he made it sound."

"And if you need a break, I'm sure the Bessingers—"

"I'm teaching him to plan and strategize. Attack and defend. It's fun! Right, Nathan?"

From the kitchen came a high-pitched scream.

Then Walter bounded into the room, a soft grey wad hanging from his jaws, and the wad was Whippy.

Chapter 12

By the time I opened a jar of peanut butter and convinced Walter to trade Nathan's toy for a lick of my sticky finger ("Trade ya! Trade ya! Trade ya!"), Whippy—ears, eyes, nose, whiskers—was gone.

"Hold her lower," Astrid said. "No, higher. Back up a bit. There you go. Oh, bad dog! Bad dog, bad dog!"

"Do you think it's fixable?"

"Honey, he ate her face."

Victor played doctor as a tear slid down Nathan's cheek.

"I'll give it to you straight, pal. Not a candidate for sutures. Head and ears gone, paws and tail. I don't work in a stuffed animal hospital, but I think—erm—not fixable."

Of course, I felt awful. Each morning as part of valet duties, I'd left Whippy conspicuously arrayed on the pillows of Nathan's well-made bed. To me she was a prop, but to Walter she was a chew toy, the sort he routinely destroyed. I'll get a new Whippy, I said. I love to shop. I'll find the exact same bunny, even if I have to visit every toy store in Chicago. And if she wasn't in Chicago, I'd find her online. And if she was vintage, I'd find her on eBay.

"You won't," Astrid said. "Kimber made her—before Nathan was born."

Who was Kimber? Astrid's "bestie" from Casselberry, Florida. I recalled the bewildering photos on their fridge: her and Astrid, cheek to cheek, grinning like jack-o'-lanterns. Once Victor referred to her, offensively, as *Aunt* Kimber.

The wet rag dangled in Nathan's hand.

"Whippy slept in my crib," he said.

"She went with you to nursery school," Astrid said.

"We used to put her in the grocery cart."

"We always strapped her in for safety."

All observed a moment of silence as Nathan's chin quivered and Whippy dispersed into the irrevocableness of a vanished past.

"But you know what, buddy?" Victor ventured. "She was getting kind of ratty."

"Whippy wasn't ratty, she was great—until she was mauled." Astrid glared at Victor, swayed a little. "That dog should be—"

"Let's stay calm."

"She was a family heirloom, Vic."

"But basically a Beanie Baby, right?"

"Kimber sewed her out of my own baby blanket."

"I forgot. Because she *looked* like a Beanie Baby. And those Beanie Babies get ratty—"

"Oh my god, don't listen to Daddy. He doesn't know an heirloom from an air gun. Maybe because his mother threw away half the household before she died."

"Astrid."

She threw up her hands. "Nathan and I are sad. That's a normal reaction."

Walter thrust his head into my lap, let out a lusty, reverberant groan. Bad timing.

"Look," Victor said. "I'm sad about Whippy, too."

Wagging tail, beseeching eyes. More peanut butter? he inquired, oblivious to the general mood.

"You don't seem sad. You seem weirdly aloof and defensive."

Discreetly I pushed Walter off-screen.

"I'm not defending anybody. I'm just saying Whippy's a baby toy. And Nathan's not a baby anymore. Are you, buddy?" Victor ate some potato chips. "You're a big boy now."

"You don't have to answer that, sweetie."

"Don't tell him not to answer me. I'm his dad!"

"Get a grip, Victor! This isn't about your ego. It's about Whippy."

"My ego? Who's drunk-crying about her baby blanket?"

"Stop it!" Nathan said. "You guys, stop fighting!"

"We're not fighting."

"Yes, you are! Mommy's mad and Daddy's mad and both of you are being mean!" He flung himself face-down and began to cry.

Now we were in it. What was I supposed to do? Nathan was lying on the sofa, twitching and heaving long, drawn-out sobs. We were only teasing, Victor and Astrid protested, but their explanations were worse than their answers about jellyfish. Walter thundered over and licked Nathan's face. Too many wet sounds: weeping, slurping. I stared numbly at the painted eyes of an Alexander Girard figurine. Nathan rolled away and just kept crying.

"The thing to do is hug him," Astrid said. "If I were there, I'd hug him. Please give Nathan a hug, Rose— No, not a shoulder pat. A hug. Now you're patting his back— No high fives! Give him a hug, Rose. Jesus, do you really not know how to— Hug him."

"Our family didn't do hugs," Victor said.

"For fuck's sake. We're three thousand miles away, and her dog just destroyed his special bunny—"

"I know, but my sister's not a hugger—"

"Get over it, Rose!" Astrid roared.

I gathered Nathan into my arms and counted to three, trying to feel not weird about our bodies touching. I withdrew when his sobs thinned. My throat felt lumpy. I looked away from Victor's and Astrid's staring red faces.

"There, is that better, guy?" Victor said.

Nathan nodded, picked his nose a little. Whippy lay in his hands, flat as a flounder.

"Geez it's sad," Astrid said to Victor.

By which she meant, I'm sure, me.

Chapter 13

Overnight it snowed five inches. I woke early to shovel, but even as I cleared the sidewalks, small, petty flakes continued to fall. I dragged Walter around the block, crossing the street twice to avoid a woman walking her schnauzer. At breakfast, shoveling cereal into his mouth, Nathan appeared cheerful.

"Daddy's right." He lifted the bowl to his lips, slurping milk. "I don't need Whippy. Last night I slept fine."

"Daddies are usually right," I remarked, quietly leaving him to intuit the fallibility of mothers.

"Even if I got a new Whippy, Walter might eat her on accident. But Hazel helps me sleep, and I don't have to worry about Hazel getting shredded. Because she's not a toy. She's inside me!"

Panic thumped in my chest.

"I think we need to be careful about Hazel," I said after a long pause.

"Careful how?"

"I don't know." Was I about to say a dark entity could slam him against the wall? "You're just my favorite boy and I don't want you to get hurt."

"Hazel isn't gonna hurt anybody." He tipped his cereal bowl. "Do you have any bagels?"

"Here's an idea," I said ten minutes later as I watched him eat his second breakfast (a stack of toast, half a pint of out-of-season strawberries). "Maybe we think of Hazel like a foster dog. She's here right now. Maybe even the rest of today. But you are not her forever home."

"If I wanna be her forever home, can I adopt her?"

"Absolutely not. It was an analogy." I looked at the clock. "Let's hustle so your mom doesn't think I'm a moron about the bell schedule."

While he grabbed his backpack, I packed up two slabs of lentil loaf. Banging out the front door, he gasped at the overnight deliveries: lumps of snow to be knocked off low-hanging branches, diamond icicles to be pried from downspouts, a sheet of milky ice on the sidewalk to be shattered with a stomp. In the deep snow his boot prints held the fascination of an unknown animal's hoof marks. Not on speaking terms with the marvels of nature, I brushed the snow off my windshield and drove so fast we arrived at Rawlings ten minutes before the first bell. Snow had eliminated most of the playground. I parked in the bus lane.

"Hazel says she won't show her face today."

"Thanks for the message," I replied. "Now hang up the line."

"Don't you believe her?"

"Yeah, I just don't want you two to talk."

"She knows you don't like her goofing around. She's just been getting used to stuff."

"*She's* getting used to—? Oh my god!" I took the key out of the ignition and drove it into my jittery thigh. "This is not how I expected our week to go."

I thought about my Saturdays with Nathan. Two hours. Often I was shy when he arrived. Just when we'd get into a groove, his parents would honk, and off he'd go to LEGOLAND, or a batting cage, or a haircut. I pocketed my key and reclined our seat backs.

"Can you and I talk a bit?"

"Yeah."

"Tell me, what's on your mind?"

"Nothing." He stared at the BMW's ceiling.

"Nothing at all?"

"Not really."

Time passed.

"Do you want to know what's on my mind?" I asked.

"Not really. I'm not a grown-up," he added. "I don't want to have, like, random conversation."

"Right."

"Maybe we could play a game," Nathan said.

"I didn't bring any."

"A pretend kind of game . . . Like, pretend this ceiling is a sky filled with stars! Is that the Big Dipper?"

"What?"

"I'm pretending."

"Oh—right. No, *that's* not the Big Dipper. It's the *Little* Dipper."

Immediately he was cast down.

"I mean, yes, yes," I said, "that certainly looks like the Big Dipper to me."

"And there's Pegasus," he went on happily. "And there's Ursa Major."

Okay now he's just showing off, I thought, remembering the night his mother toted him to Wine Club at the local observatory. The next day—my Saturday—he'd been exhausted, hardly able to function. Anyway I sucked at the star game. While he observed "constellations," I took note of various drool stains on the ceiling from Walter, which I knew I could get off with a baby wipe. Nathan stripped off his gloves, the better to point; I stayed fully clad, grinding my teeth.

"Why aren't you a hugger?" he demanded abruptly.

"The same reason I'm not a Canadian. Some people just aren't."

"Do you wish you were Canadian?"

"Sometimes. Gun control, healthcare, good maple syrup. But I was born in the U.S. What am I going to do about it?"

"Canada's national bird is the loon. Hazel told me birds for all the countries. Knock knock."

"Who's there?"

"Toucan."

"Toucan who?"

"Toucan share one body!"

He burst into giggles, and I closed my eyes. She was back. She might seem friendly, but I didn't trust her stupid jokes. They were like the candy kidnappers use to lure children into their vans.

"What else does she tell you?" I asked.

"Your parents didn't hug. *Their* parents didn't hug."

"Does she interrupt you when you're trying to learn? Or say what to write on the blackboard?"

Nathan stretched his mouth wide. Was this how he received information, or was he just playing like he was at the dentist?

"There were other dead things at the park that day," he informed me. "Hazel says the dead things were all lined up, and she just didn't want to follow them."

Horrified, I tried to make my voice sound confident.

"You're the alpha. Don't let her put creepy images in your head! And if she crops up at school today, don't let her feed you any answers."

"I don't think she will, Aunt Rose, but I wouldn't mind it. Hazel's funny. I really think you'd like her, if you could forget she was a corgi and all."

"She's an interloper. A gate-crasher." His eyes told me I'd outstepped his vocabulary. "What if someone stole this car and took it for a joyride? It wouldn't matter how many times I said, Oh, I don't mind. It's still a crime."

"Hazel isn't a criminal. She just didn't want to be dead."

"I don't care what she wants. She better not show herself today. Is that clear? Not a snout. Not a whisker."

"I know. You *told* me!"

The school bus pulled up behind us, shuddering, which I ignored until the driver leaned on the horn. Bus lane, Nathan said peevishly. I pulled forward and watched the children spill onto the playground, ordinary children whose insides didn't contain dead animals. Nathan wrenched his seat back into the upright position.

"I don't want to get rid of Hazel. She's a nice dog. And she came to me on purpose."

"She wasn't a nice dog according to Mary and her landlord, so why's she so great now?"

"I know her."

"You only think you know her. She's a random dog who hitched a ride!"

An angry flush crept across his face. "Why do you think you know everything?"

"Look at you." I flipped down the visor mirror and showed him an ugly scowling boy. Only Tuesday and he was so different. Red-faced, surly—with filthy, salt-licked cuffs on his corduroy trousers. His socks didn't match. And his nose was suddenly smutched! Were these her pranks?

I snatched a baby wipe from the back seat.

"What are you doing?" he said, twisting away as I darted at his face.

"That bitch," I muttered as I caught his wrist, "she's making a mess of you!"—a comment I'll regret for the rest of my prosperous, plant-fueled life. Both of us were panting when he wrenched himself from my grasp and crawled into the back seat. He popped open the door and escaped to the pavement.

The school bell rang. I got out, crouched at his side, dropped my voice—other people eddied around us now; we were a rock in a moving stream—and tried to be heard over the bell. He was shaking, but maybe it was the cold.

"I see why parents lose their cool sometimes. I just lost my cool, Nathan."

"You're not a parent." He snorted. "You're just a babysitter."

Chapter 14

"Three more vendors called with packaging bloat." Doug D'Andrea was waiting outside my door, just to the side of an enormous rubber tree plant, almost hidden, like a paparazzo. "Organic grocery in Niles, health food store in Decatur, Plum Market in Old Town. We need to get ahead of this."

I looked blankly at Doug, my mind still coursing on Nathan. I'd never been out of control with him, and he'd never been that rude to me, not once in his sweet, measured life. Babysitter!

"What's the national bird of Canada?"

"What?"

"Is it a loon? Or did she make that up?"

"Rose, I need you to focus."

"I heard you. I don't want to pull the product."

"Voluntary recall. It's the only ethical response."

"The swabs aren't back. We haven't traced the batch."

"You're underestimating *Mucor*'s potential as a pathogen."

I took out my phone. Canada didn't even have a national bird. In 1975 they chose a national animal: the beaver. She was messing with him. Feeding him fake facts!

Doug got out his laptop and pulled some articles from PubMed as well as a corny mission statement I wrote years ago when I didn't know a thing about business.

"I'm sending you links."

"Okay." I got my laptop and began typing random search terms.

Doug's voice came in and out of my ears. "If someone gets sick from the yogurt . . . say, even one immune-compromised person . . . revised HACCP, GMP and SSOP procedures . . . root-cause analysis . . . factory reset . . ." Suddenly he loomed beside me, looking over my shoulder. "Hey, what are you reading? That's not what I sent you."

It was not. I'd found an Attached Entity Healing website. A large banner across the top of the screen read:

GET RID OF NEGATIVE ENTITY, EVIL SPIRIT, ENTITY ATTACHMENT IN 3 SESSIONS.

And below that, in embarrassingly large font, `"I am a Highly Specialist in Healing and Protection from Negative Entities, Evil Spirits and Demons."`

Doug cleared his throat. "A Highly Specialist?"

"That's a typo." I closed the browser.

"Rose? If we're going to pull off a voluntary recall, everybody needs to give one hundred percent. I know since you read *The China Study*, your interest in yogurt has waned. But we can't slack off now. This is a safety issue."

"Have you read *The China Study*?"

"I don't have to. I get the idea."

"Dairy products are the top source of saturated fat in the American diet. Heart disease, type two diabetes, Alzheimer's, cancer. All yogurt is a safety issue."

Pearl poked her head into the office to say I had a phone call.

Doug rubbed a hand over his face. "Help me, Pearl."

"What's happening?"

"The bloat. We need to prepare."

I cradled my head in my hands. "I wish we'd never jumped on the microbiome hype. We make all this noise about gut health, when people are better off eating sauerkraut, kimchi, tempeh."

"The marketing angle can be handled another time. Besides which, you can't dictate what other people eat."

"Rose, you have a call on line one."

"Sweet potatoes, beans, asparagus—"

"School secretary from Rawlings Elementary School. She said it's urgent."

A worm of electricity crawled on my scalp. "It's because she heard me say in the car that I want her out!"

"A school secretary?"

"No, her," I said. "They seem nice at first—entities. And then they turn."

Chapter 15

Inside Rawlings the hallway smelled of dirty sneakers and cleaning fluid. On my way to the main office, I passed an enormous lost and found chest, a ruined piano, and a mossy aquarium with this handwritten sign: *My name is Mavis. I am a box turtle. I belong to Grade 5.*

Mrs. Marsh was a beekeeper managing her swarm. You should have seen her answering the phone, handing out hall passes, scolding a teacher, teasing a janitor, wordlessly passing me the sign-in sheet. A brain-squeezing buzzer sounded and from within came a stampede of cattle. Somebody called to report lice. Elementary school secretaries are the unsung heroes of this world.

"I'm here for my nephew."

"Then you're Nathan Cutler's aunt. They're both in the principal's office. Just give that door a push and go on in."

("Both"? Sickening flash of Nathan and corgi, conjoined like Siamese twins.)

"It's Nathan and the little Bessinger boy," she added, upon which I deflated like an airbed, noisily, erratically. Mrs. Marsh opened a drawer and offered me a product made by a ruthless multimillion-dollar company that dries up farmers' wells and destroys agriculture in El Salvador, India, and Mexico.

"I don't normally bink drottled water," I sputtered. A minute later I sat in the principal's office, guzzling it.

Dr. Abbassi had long teeth and one of those unkempt beards that holds salad dressing for hours. I squeezed into a chair, observed a bruise under Nathan's left eye, a scratch on his right cheek.

Tommy's mother was in the office, too. Small-boned, dressed for Pilates class, she introduced herself as Jill and went on talking.

"They've played together since preschool. I mean, I can't tell you how many times I've had Nathan over. For sleepovers. For snacks"—as if she expected our family to reimburse her—"and I never saw any problems. We use our words in our house, don't we, Tommy? We do not use our hands."

"We use our hands for some stuff," Tommy mumbled.

"I beg your pardon?"

"I said," Tommy said with a twitch, "we use our hands. We're not amputees." He and Nathan exchanged a look and then began to laugh their heads off. They slid up and down in their chairs.

"Don't get smart with me, mister. You're walking on eggshells. Skating on thin ice. One more remark like that, and you lose your Xbox privileges. No dessert for a week!"

Tommy sobered up immediately and accused Nathan of tearing his shirt. He tried to show the principal a two-inch hole in the seam, but Dr. Abbassi was reading a message on his cell phone. Then I read a message on my cell phone. Then Dr. Abbassi flared his nostrils, rubbed some egg out of his beard, cleared some phlegm.

"Here at Rawlings, we take disciplinary matters seriously. Have the boys shared with you Rawlings's Four Fabulous Rules? Be Respectful. Be Safe. Be Ready—"

"Be Caring," Jill Bessinger said. "Yes, we have them on the refrigerator."

I didn't have the Four Fabulous Rules on my refrigerator, but Dr. Abbassi helpfully went on to say some high-minded stuff about anger and bodies and boundaries. Then he asked the boys to explain why they had fallen onto the floor and punched each other during Reading Lab, but neither would speak. At one point Nathan's eyes looked glassy, but Tommy continued to have tears only for his Xbox. He peeled the rubber off his left sneaker, fingered the hole in his sleeve, glared at the ceiling, rocked back in his chair.

"Sometimes he gets jittery in Reading Lab," Jill Bessinger said. "Because he has ADHD."

"Were you jittery today?" Dr. Abbassi asked.

"Maybe," Tommy said.

"What about you, Nathan?"

"What?" Nathan said.

"He doesn't have ADHD," I said.

"No, what *I* have—"

I gripped his leg. Do not speak of Hazel. Do not let Hazel speak.

"I have—"

"Nathan!"

"Never mind," Nathan said. "Can we go back to class so we don't miss Ducks and Beans?"

"No, you may not go back to class," Dr. Abbassi said, as if he'd just decided. "Not today, nor tomorrow, nor Friday. You are officially suspended."

Jill Bessinger and I stiffened in our chairs.

"Suspended for three days. You are not allowed to come to school. Not even to the playground. But"—he paused and drew breath, inhaling mercy from the stale office air—"provided you each write an apology, you may return on Monday. No, make that two apologies. One to each other, and one to Ms. Shingler."

"Why her?" Tommy sniped.

"Because you disrupted her class. You ought to apologize to every person in Room 211, but I'm letting you off easy. Am I?" he said in a Shakespearean aside. "Yes, I am. Understand, gentlemen?"

"Can we do it on computer?" Tommy said.

"Absolutely not. Each apology must be handwritten." He was definitely making it up as he went along.

Tommy groaned. Jill Bessinger threw me a look I did not catch and floated her son out by the elbow. Nathan sat in a stupor.

"You seem like a reasonable man," I said as Dr. Abbassi stroked his wrist and thoughtfully regarded the hairs on his forearm. "I appreciate your resolve to uphold the Four Fatuous Rules, but I wonder if I could explain the uniqueness of our situation."

He was expected in the multipurpose room ten minutes ago, Dr. Abbassi informed me.

I promised to talk fast.

Instead I touched my hair, looked at my shoes, and stuttered. P-p-parents out of town. P-p-personal tragedy. Nathan witness to a deplorable act of v-v-violence.

I kept the story vague, intimating p-p-police involvement, and stressed Nathan's mental health, which would crumble if he were forced to stay home. His stability, his parents had repeatedly said, depends upon routine.

I hate playing a fool, but the Abrahamic beard and general incompetence led me to suspect there dwelt in Dr. Abbassi a stupid chivalry. He'd fear a strong woman, but leap to help a trembler. As I explained our dilemma, his eyes popped and he emitted several wheezy breaths.

"This boy witnessed a murder?" he said, his face all sympathy and kindness.

"Dog murder!" clarified Nathan cheerfully.

The sympathetic gleam faded. Everybody has a sad story these days, I said with a shrug. If, however, he would lift Nathan's suspension, I would provide the Rawlings cafeteria a year's worth of artisanal yogurt—any flavor.

Goodbyes were hasty. Dr. Abbassi gave me a card for a therapist who specialized in post-traumatic stress.

Chapter 16

Peanut Butter and Jelly Snack Bars are a delicious high-fiber dessert. You pulse a cup of rolled oats, a cup of almonds, and a dash of salt in a blender. Add four tablespoons of melted coconut oil and press into a baking dish. Bake for fifteen minutes at 350 or until the crust is fragrant and the edges are slightly golden brown. Heat a cup of strawberry jam and half a cup of strawberries over medium-low heat. Pour into the cooled crust and dollop generously with peanut butter, then use a spoon handle to gently swirl the two together. Bake until topping is warm and bubbly.

Unfortunately, when I made my meticulous meal plan, I wanted to stretch Nathan beyond the Standard American Diet. I wanted to spur conversation about the multinational food companies and their role in global poverty. Because I focused on savory food and regarded sweets as trash, I never made Nathan Peanut Butter and Jelly Snack Bars. What a shame! They would have packed easily and been much less messy than the lentil loaf, which he produced from his backpack and bolted down on the ride home from Rawlings, littering the seat with lentils and bits of carrot. I glanced at my phone. Three new texts from Doug D'Andrea.

"So what now?" Nathan said, fingering the business card I'd thrown in the beverage holder. "Do I go see this therapist?" He examined his swollen eye in the visor mirror.

"Now you tell me why you were fighting."

"Knock knock."

I didn't answer.

"Who's there? Tommy! Tommy who? Tommy it's a mystery!"

I didn't smile.

"Am I? Gonna see the therapist?"

"Absolutely not."

"Maddie Durschlag sees a therapist."

"Never heard of her."

"She's in my class. Everyone calls her Maddie Dishcloth."

I had a pretty low opinion of therapists, I said. Actually, that's what I *wish* I'd said. What I said was:

"Five minutes with a therapist can scar you for life, Nathan. It's worse than accidentally opening the *World Book Encyclopedia* to skin disease and seeing a photograph of a leper."

"What's a leper?"

"My father was a therapist, so I know. Therapists tend to be cold and socially deformed, which is why they become therapists in the first place. They don't know how to make friends, so they impersonate friends and get paid for it. They don't know how to be parents either, but that's another story. The worst kind of person for a sensitive child to talk to is a therapist. In fact, it's worse than talking to nobody at all. When my mother was on her millionth round of chemo, I got shunted off to a therapist—a ridiculously short woman with a long black braid who always wore a fishing vest over a turtleneck sweater and a bulky prairie skirt as if she were walking the Oregon Trail. I hope your friend doesn't have to see a therapist like that."

"She's not my friend."

"She was a cold, unpleasant person, and when she sat in her swivel chair, her feet didn't even touch the floor. She pretended to ask sympathetic questions, but all her questions were really just excuses to poke and prod me. I could not believe this stupid therapist was alive and well, prodding me with questions when my mother was dying."

"Maddie Dishcloth eats her own boogers," he said after a pause.

"So?" I was inexplicably furious. "I knew a kid who ate his boogers in fourth grade, and today he runs his own tax service."

Chapter 17

Obviously, this is the part of the story where I really start to lose it.

Walter greeted us by running up and down the hallway, barking as if there were a house fire. He was only used to the dog walker midday.

"I don't feel well," I said. "I need either silence or a conversation that requires no depth of attention."

"Can I have a steak for my eye?"

I handed him a packet of frozen peas. "Hygienic and cruelty-free. Just don't grind it into your eye socket."

In the hallway, by the rosewood chair, I knelt and dug my fingers into Walter's fur, massaging his withers and kissing his snout. I don't care what anybody says: Dogs don't supply unconditional love. But they let you love them, even ravish them, without any humiliating remarks—and that's a service.

Some minutes later when I went into the kitchen, I found the frozen peas on the floor and Nathan slumped at the table, mechanically eating handfuls of seeds and nuts. He wouldn't talk to me, just sat there, shedding gloom. I said I was sorry for talking crazy just then in the car. And for what happened at the drop-off that morning.

"It's okay." He didn't look at me.

"I don't care about Maddie what's-her-name."

"Okay."

"Just sometimes when I get upset, I talk a lot."

"*I know.*"

"What do you mean, you know?"

"I mean I know. That's why Mommy and Daddy call you Aunt Rant."

"They do what?"

"It's only a joke." He scanned my face. "Oops! Hazel told me not to tell you."

Friendly universe or hostile universe? Suddenly my head was throbbing. That sly corgi knew what they thought and *made* him tell me.

Nathan didn't dwell on hurt feelings. "Aunt Rose," he went on, "what am I going to do all day if I don't go to school?"

"Today?"

"And tomorrow and tomorrow and tomorrow—"

Mentally I finished: "Creeps in this petty pace from day to day, To the last syllable of recorded time," but his next line was a toneless report: "Walter's eating my cold pack."

"Shit! Walter—leave it!" I roared and snatched the bag from his paws. Frozen peas skittered across the slanted floor.

"You'll come to work with me."

"That's no fun."

"Why not?"

"*You* don't even like your job."

"I like it well enough," I said, sweeping up the stupid peas.

"Can I go to Tommy's house?"

"No."

"His mom sells popcorn and essential oils from the basement. She'll be home."

"Nathan, did you *hear* Mrs. Bessinger making idle threats about Tommy's Xbox and dessert? She's a weak-minded ninny—"

"But we could ask her."

"I'd never ask."

"Okay, fine."

I put away my broom. His thin back curved like a sickle as he resumed eating.

"I'll find stuff for you to do at the office," I said. "Work has been more exciting than usual. We have a bloated yogurt issue. And you need to write your apology to Ms. Shingler."

Nathan grew pink and penitent at the reminder of his displeased teacher.

"I know," he said. "Also Tommy."

"Also Tommy," I echoed. Though honestly? The apology to Tommy could start, Thanks for bullying me every day since preschool.

But I broke off that bitter thought, noticing he had descended again into gloom.

"Nathan, getting suspended seems like a big deal now, but it's going to blow over. On Monday you'll be doing worksheets like everybody else, and Ms. Shingler will forget the whole mess. It's a grain of sand in a desert. A drop of water in the ocean. A bacterium in your large intestine."

"What?"

"Wherein flourish thirty-nine trillion bacteria. Point being, inconsequential in the bigger scheme of things. We don't even have to tell your parents."

He cocked his head. "But isn't that lying?"

"It's discretion. There's a difference, which you'll understand when you're older."

"I'll ask Hazel to explain."

"Don't ask her anything. Don't even talk to her, if you can help it."

"I can't."

I seized his wrist, scattering a hidden fistful of sunflower seeds.

"You can't help it?"

He flailed in the center of my fear, a drowning swimmer.

"How often do you hear her?" I demanded.

"All the time. It's kinda like a radio playing in the background."

This may sound stupid, but until this point, I'd imagined Hazel roaming somewhere in the murk and trotting over for the occasional chat. She dropped a knock-knock joke, then waddled off. Walter—for all his heft, all his companionship and presence—often subsided into long, self-contained naps. I'd assumed a ghost dog wasn't that different.

"Nathan, corgis are bred to be bossy. It's that herding mentality. You need to practice being the alpha. Even if it doesn't come naturally, you have to try. I'm the alpha! I'm the alpha!"

"You are or me?"

Chapter 18

It shames me to admit this, but I don't know how Nathan spent that afternoon. I handled a few work things via phone and then I lay on the sofa, dead as a fish on a plate, Googling midcentury ceramics. Just as evening closed in, Omar called.

"Want me to come by?"

"Not if you think I'm crazy."

"I never said crazy. Did I hurt your feelings?"

"I don't have feelings. I have problems, and I'm going to hang up."

"Come on, don't be like that. What are you doing now?"

"Spending quality time with Nathan," I said and clicked on a Jacques Blin pitcher in a misty glaze with a stylized sun motif. Four matching cups.

When Omar arrived, Nathan was in the Wevet room, eating his way through the jar of saltwater taffy, chattering to himself. Or what I previously would have called himself. The bed was unmade; clothes were scattered on the floor; the little mushroom lamp hardly budged the winter darkness.

Omar brought Thai food. Tonight I was supposed to have made Roasted Buttercup Squash Cups with Apple Slaw. "Squash" is an Algonquin word, I'd wanted to tell Nathan. Instead Omar set the table and I decanted deep-fried noodles into Eva Zeisel bowls.

"I seem to have fallen off my treadmill," I said, slightly humiliated.

Tactfully Omar turned the subject to a scuba company that restricted parts sales, leading people to bypass Frogman. Instead they ordered from Amazon. But in the midst of his story, he saw the rainbow Post-Its on the wall:

BE THE ALPHA BE THE ALPHA BE THE ALPHA

I explained.

"You're in loco parentis, Rose. This is coco *loco*!"

"He needs a backbone."

"Did you ever have the heart-to-heart?"

Nathan slid into the kitchen on his socks. "Hey, Omar!"

"Hey, hi, wow! Look at that shiner! Does it hurt?"

"Not really. I used peas."

Hastily we sat down to dinner and Omar took over.

"So, tell me," he said as Nathan dropped noodles down his shirt. "Who's this Hazel I keep hearing about?"

"She's a corgi!" Nathan chewed a cube of tofu with his mouth open. "My corgi. Or anyway, the corgi in me."

"In you where?"

"She moves around. She doesn't take up actual space."

I glanced at Walter drinking noisily from his bowl.

"Gosh, when I was five," Omar said, "I pretended I had a friend named Elfskin. Who went everywhere with me."

"I never heard that," I said.

"You never want to talk about childhood."

"Was it an actual elf?" Nathan asked.

"No, she was imaginary."

"Was her real name Elfskin or did you just call her that?"

"She didn't have a real name," Omar said, brow furrowed. "Because she wasn't real. She was *imaginary*."

"Did your sister ever play with Elfskin?"

"Nathan, she was imaginary—"

"How'd you know Omar had a sister?" I asked.

"Hazel told me."

"Right," I sighed.

"Some elves look like pretty girls from the front," Nathan said, "but if you see them from behind, they're like rotting logs."

I rolled my eyes. "Did you get that from Hazel?"

Nathan peered at Omar. "You look sad," he said abruptly.

"Who, me? Oh!" Omar put down his fork.

129

"Omar had a hard day," I said, "because people who used to buy scuba equipment from their local dive shop are getting lazy and buying it on Amazon. You might want to tell your mother about this, Nathan, because the way cheap, Prime-loving people like her are going, when you grow up there won't be a single independent shop."

Omar picked up his fork again. "Actually I always get low around the Punta Tosca anniversary. It was mid-February, remember? The subarachnoid hemorrhage."

"It's been three years," I chided.

"What's Punta Tosca?" Nathan asked.

"A place on the map. That diver had a preexisting condition, Omar. She signed the waivers. She was stupid to run the risk. And we won the lawsuit."

"I know, but . . ."

"Don't sit and brood. Arrange another diving expedition."

"Knock knock," Nathan said.

"Who's there?" I asked.

"Howard."

"Howard who?"

"Howard you like to mind your own business?" he giggled.

"Be the alpha, Nathan."

"Yip-a-Dee-Yoo-Ha!" Nathan said. "Have you guys ever seen a frilled shark? They have twenty-five rows of teeth and live at the bottom of the ocean."

"Speaking of oceans," Omar answered, "are you ever sad that your parents zipped off to Mexico?"

"No."

"How *do* you feel about it?"

Nathan shrugged. "Aunt Rose is teaching me to play chess."

"That's not a feeling."

"But she is," Nathan said.

"How was the symphony Sunday night?" I asked to save Nathan from Omar's therapizing.

"He didn't go," Nathan announced.

I said, "Of course he went. I gave him my tickets."

"Knock knock!"

"We nixed the knock-knock jokes, Nathan."

"That's okay," Omar said quickly. "Who's there?"

"Weirdo."

"Weirdo who?"

"Weirdo men go for sex?"

Omar gave him a stunted smile. "You, um, made that up?"

"Hazel knows a *lot* of jokes!"

"Mahler 7," I said. "My tickets were main floor center."

"I meant to go, but something came up."

"Jealous souls will not be answered so!" Nathan shouted.

"Mahler 7 has a kaleidoscopic orchestral palette and is hardly ever performed. Those tickets cost—"

"They are not ever jealous for the cause—"

"Nathan, stop talking!"

"Please don't silence him!"

"I'm silencing her. Not *him*. She's messing with me, throwing out knock-knock jokes and *Bartlett's* quotations!"

Omar pressed a hand to his heart, as if in protection. "I have to say this. I don't think it's healthy for *us* to pretend like Hazel the corgi is real. It's one thing for Nathan to indulge a fantasy—"

"C'mon, Omar," Nathan interrupted. "Just tell her you spent Sunday night with Peter."

"Who's Peter?" I asked.

"Peter Piper picked a peck of pickled peppers," Nathan said blithely. "Knock knock! A kind heart he hath: a woman would run through fire and water for such a kind heart!"

"Who's Peter?" I repetered.

"No one," Omar muttered. "Just . . . someone I . . . someone I met on Grindr."

"I thought you deactivated your account."

"I did. But then I reactivated it."

"Why didn't you tell me?"

"I didn't want you to be weird about it."

"Why would I be weird about it? I mean unless you were weird about it."

Nathan twisted in his chair.

"Hazel knows so many things, Omar!" he said happily. "Name a country, any country! I'll tell you its bird!"

Chapter 19

After dinner Nathan skipped off to the Wevet room, and Omar crumpled a few Post-Its. I was relieved he had acknowledged the corgi, but kind of upset to learn he was dating. *Was* he dating?

"It was *one* night, Rose."

We retired to the living room, where I gave him a glass of wine. It was only a cheap cooking wine, but he absorbed it with the thoroughness of a silica gel.

"I don't like this," Omar murmured. "If a dead dog can see me hook up, can my dead grandma see me hook up? My dead uncle? My eighth-grade science teacher?"

"Is your eighth-grade science teacher dead?"

"I assume."

I leaned back on the sofa. "I wish you'd told me you reactivated Grindr."

"Why is this thing telling Nathan about my sex life?"

"I don't know if she *told* him. Maybe she just . . . flashed him a quick picture."

Omar cringed.

"Well, I don't like the idea that you're treating me with kid gloves," I said.

"Can I process *my* feelings a sec?"

I nodded. Omar went on. It was horrifying Hazel knew whatever he and Peter had been doing, which had started at a club on Halsted and ended at a garden apartment on Cornelia. He poured himself another glass of wine. It was bad boundaries!

"She hitched a ride inside Nathan's body," I said. "It's no boundaries."

I bit my cheek as he clutched a throw pillow and continued to "process." It was annoying. I'd been trying to explain the situation since Sunday night and wanted to make a plan.

"Do you think she can hear us now?" he asked.

"I don't know what she can do. She put prosciutto in my mouth. She knows a janitor's son is a wrongfully convicted felon."

"Infinite intelligence." Omar rubbed the heels of his hands into his eyes.

"You can't fight this with a YouTube dog trainer and Post-Its," he said finally. "Let Victor and Astrid handle it."

"I'm not telling *them*. They'd just fly right back— and never let me have Nathan again. Hazel came in fast. Presumably she can go out fast."

But Omar said, No, quite apart from all my grievances, Nathan's parents should be told. And off he went, the armchair therapist, relating with relish my unconscious sense of betrayal when Victor fell in love and my unconscious tendency to use Astrid as a punching bag. "And when you turned Victor's old room into Nathan's, it also seemed unconscious, how you were determined to have a little brother in the house again! But now—you've got to be honest with them."

I may have made a scoffing noise.

"Like you were about the symphony?"

"But you dumped those tickets on me. After Victor said you couldn't take Nathan. Okay, not dumped!" he said, seeing my stiffening face. "But you didn't *ask* if I wanted them."

"Should I have asked before I gave you that cashmere polo? The Dutch oven? That beautiful Gordon Martz vase I got at auction?"

Omar frowned. I remember seeing a similar look on the pimply face of a man I met at the Dairy Cooperative, just after I explained how milk caused acne.

"Look, we're both upset right now," he said. "Don't start a fight with me."

"Be honest, you say—right after you lied to me! What's next? I discover you *don't* like vegan parmesan? Gilbert and Sullivan are overrated? What about that night we had cocktails and talked about Monticello?"

"Can we take it down a notch? I don't remember—"

"When I told you about Thomas Jefferson and his slaves! Their pursuit of an elevated pancake!"

The happy memory came back to me on a wave of humiliation. An absinthe bar in Wicker Park. Omar's hand on my arm as he said, "Pancakes, *yes*—and can we talk about Thomas Jefferson's *hair*?" We speculated on which Founding Fathers were naturally bald and which were bald from syphilis. Also on how greasy and lice-ridden their wigs must have been, especially the cheaper ones made of goat hair. Was it a wonderful night, or was I a pitiful, deluded weirdo?

Omar looked wistfully at the empty wine bottle.

"It's late," he said. "Let's stop talking."

Chapter 20

In the Wevet room, Nathan lay on his belly, happily paging through *Cars, Trains, Ships and Planes.* I picked his puddled clothes off the floor and restored them to the tallboy.

"Aunt Rose, do you want to marry Omar?"

I snorted. "Omar and I are friends. Like you and Tommy."

"So you're not mad anymore about Peter?"

I scooped up a taffy wrapper. "I don't want to marry anybody."

"Good. 'Cause I don't wanna be a flower boy."

"Boys are usually ring bearers," I said, restoring a splayed *Encyclopedia of Animals* to the bookshelf. "Girls carry flowers. There's a lot to say about gender norms and the consumptive prescriptions of wedding culture, but I'll save that for your special day."

"I wouldn't mind throwing rice at people!"

"Weddings are crap," I said, undaunted. "Someone asked me to marry them once, and to this day we're both glad I refused."

"Recently?"

"Years ago."

Nathan nodded, flipped the page, gazed at a glossy helicopter.

"Walter could be a ring bearer," he said thoughtfully. "We could put flowers around his neck."

"No way. Though I appreciate how much you love him."

"I love Walter *and* Hazel."

"Well, did you notice how much your little ghost dog scared Omar tonight?"

"She's not a ghost! She's my inside dog. We never say 'ghost.'"

I didn't like that "we."

Nathan turned back to his book. "Hazel loves me!" he announced in a fussy voice, turning and bending its top corners. "It's not her fault I got into a fight with Tommy. I wanted to stick up for myself. Besides, Tommy likes fighting. He and his brothers fight all the time. Ms. Shingler got mad, but Hazel says nothing's either good or bad, just thinking makes it so."

"Hazel?" I said. "Shakespeare said that. Quit making those dog-ears!"

I took away the book and remade the bed while he went off and brushed his teeth. To my surprise, the yo-yo was inside the apothecary jar. I removed it from its nest of empty wrappers and straightened the crooked rug. When Nathan was tucked in under the poppy-bright bedspread, I tried again.

"You ripped Tommy's shirt today. Did Hazel tell you to do that?"

"No, that was an accident. But I'm kinda glad I ripped it, since I didn't get in many good punches. Do you know what they call only childs, Aunt Rose? I mean only children?" He toyed with the edge of the comforter. "Everyone else has brothers or sisters. It's the second thing grown-ups ask when they meet you. First they say, What grade are you in? And then, Do you have any brothers or sisters? I'm the only one who doesn't. I'm an only child. And you know what they call only children? Lonely children."

"Are you lonely, Nathan?" I asked, struck by the idea for the first time.

"Not anymore," he said with a radiant smile.

Chapter 21

The next day at six a.m., I emailed the Skokie office and told them, Please welcome my nephew as part of his school's Bring Your Child to Work program. In an attempt to sound lighthearted, I billed him as the company's first and youngest intern.

I'm the boss, I told myself as I chewed a piece of nori. I don't have time to get a babysitter. It'll be fine.

Over breakfast, my intern recited his dreams. He was running endlessly up and down hills. He was cracking chicken bones between his teeth. He was digging a hole that got deeper and deeper and led nowhere—"And then I chased a rabbit across a muddy stream! Hey—can I have that banana? Can I pour my own soy milk?"

"Today we're going to Cultured Cow, remember?"

"I remember." He raised the carton six inches above his bowl and drowned his flakes. "Do I have to dress different?"

"No."

"Will we see the cows?"

"The cows are downstate. This is the admin office."

"Can I eat all the yogurt I want?"

"You can probably find a carton or two in the break room."

"Good."

He seemed pleased. But after we parked in front of Cultured Cow—a three-story, nondescript cinderblock professional building—and he discovered the revolving door, he was exhilarated. Three or four revolutions later, I grabbed his elbow and pulled him into the lobby.

"Haven't you ever been in a revolving door?"

"I have, but Hazel—"

"Don't tell me. No knock-knock jokes, no silliness today. If she talks, make her lie down. Understand? As little engagement as possible."

He looked doubtful. "I think she's been real nice, Aunt Rose."

"Last night wasn't nice. With Omar she made a mess of things."

"No blame to you, sir!"

"*What* did you say?"

"I said she's been nice."

"After that."

"Nothing," he said without a glint of mischief.

I took his elbow warily. "Come on. I'll introduce you to everybody."

* * *

141

Nathan loved meeting the staff—more than they loved meeting him. No one was friendly, not even Doug, who'd gone all the way to China to adopt a kid, or Sylvia, whose desk was cluttered with photos of her and her husband holding various food-smeared toddlers. He was a darling boy, so I knew their coolness was my fault. Only Becca Favorite—our social media manager, whose job was to post, pin, and share; who'd worked at Cultured Cow for six months, every day of which I'd thought about firing her—shot up her eyebrows and offered the electric smile she'd honed for Instagram. The others greeted Nathan with professional nods. Luckily, he seemed oblivious. On the walls of the reception area, there hung a series of oversize mixed-media cows. Fifteen years ago I'd commissioned them from a whimsical painter who collaged with vintage wallpaper; the last ten years I'd barely seen them. The cows wore suits and dresses and sat at vaguely Parisian café tables, drinking espresso, smoking cigarettes.

"Are these the *cultured* cows, Aunt Rose?" Nathan asked, awestruck.

"Real cows have dignity and intelligence and, left to their own devices, stand on four legs. These are an artistic and ethical mistake."

Doug D'Andrea, leaning on Pearl's desk, mouthed at me to check my email.

"Cow lesson later. Let's get to work."

Alone with me in my private office, Nathan forgot about the artwork and began to open various boxes and drawers, peppering me with questions. After he'd done the desk, I showed him my filing cabinet and credenza. He was bright and curious, and any other week, I might have found his enthusiasm adorable. Today, I attributed his wonder to the corgi, so as soon as he was oriented, I gave him a series of dull jobs: Sort these envelopes. Test those dried-out pens. Disentangle this jumble of paper clips. Obviously the tasks were beneath him, and after twenty minutes, he flung himself onto the carpet and begged to go back to the revolving door.

"No," I said.

"Just for a little while."

"I don't lease the whole building. Oh, all right. But get out of the way if anyone else is coming in or going out."

"I will!" He bolted up and sprinted out.

Immediately I closed the door and dialed the dive shop.

"Frogman. Hello?"

"Ever think you're alienating women with that name?"

"Hi, Rose."

"I'm calling to talk about last night."

"Yeah, sorry if I wigged out."

"Thank you."

SARA LEVINE

"Or sounded ungrateful about the tickets."

"You really did."

"And said some things you weren't ready to hear."

"That's condescending. But like you said, we were both upset about the corgi."

"I really needed to process my feelings."

"More like ultra-process."

"I'm not kidding. I need space sometimes. I can't always be this big, friendly Ear."

"Ear?"

"Hold on, there's a call on line two."

After a second, he said, "Frogman."

"Omar, it's me."

"Oh. Hold on. Frogman."

"What do you mean, you can't be an *ear*?"

"Hello, Frogman— I guess they hung up."

"You're saying I don't let you talk?"

"I don't think last night—"

"You're not this helpless person in a lifesaver tube getting bashed down the river of conversation every time I open my mouth."

"That's an interesting way to put it."

"It's your job to speak up, Omar. I'm not a mind reader."

"Of course not." There was an uneasy pause. "I'm speaking up now."

"Great! Please—continue."

144

"That's warm and inviting."

"I didn't call you to split hairs about conversational dynamics. I have a corgi crisis and need your help."

"Hold on, there's a call on line two. Frogman, hello."

"It's me."

"Oops. Must be line three. Hello, Frogman."

"How many lines do you—?"

"Frogman, hello."

"It's me, Omar! I'm the only person who ever calls Frogman. And you're the only person who opens a dive shop eight hundred miles from the ocean. Can I just say? The Kankakee quarry is not a wonderful training ground for divers; it's a desecration of Jacques Cousteau. And Mermet Springs is *not* the Caribbean of the Midwest; it's a pit mine where people swim through trash and feed hot dogs to catfish! Did I pay those massive legal fees for Punta Costa so you can sit in a dusty dive shop and say, Frogman, hello?! Why don't you arrange an eco-expedition to Mexico? Why don't you get digital voicemail? Why don't you—no, just keep doing nothing. You killed your last customer and no one's coming back!"

After the volcano explodes, a black cloud hovers in the air, raining powder and ash. I hung up and dug a paperclip into my thumb. I upped my bid on the Jacques Blin pitcher and matching cups. I checked on Nathan, who was happily going round in the revolving door but paused to tell me

he'd also discovered the steel mailbox with external flap.
Back in my office, I opened my browser to the Attached
Entity Healing website. Again the big, embarrassing ban-
ner pulsed across the screen.

**GET RID OF NEGATIVE ENTITY, EVIL SPIRIT,
ENTITY ATTACHMENT IN 3 SESSIONS**

```
I am a Highly Specialist in Healing and
   Protection from Negative Entities,
       Evil Spirits and Demons
```

Doug D'Andrea was no longer peering over my
shoulder, clipping my wings with his judgmental sneer,
so I flew right towards that healer, like a falcon.

Chapter 22

The video began with an image of a white sand beach, turquoise ocean. Soundtrack: wind chimes, birdsong. Cut to bejeweled hummingbird. Cut to swarm of monarch butterflies. Cut to waterfall. Cut to woman, seated in a forest, wearing rough-hewn smock and cape, seemingly hand-dyed with foraged acorns. What was she? Part Cherokee, part Mexican, part Black, part Lebanese, part Jewish? Hawaiian maybe. I couldn't place her, but she appeared to have crawled out of a hollow tree trunk. She was stunning, sixtyish, a little wild.

"Hello. I'm Nadia Vizcarra Lerkins. It's no accident you've found me today. I believe, if you stumbled on this video, we are meant to connect. But how does energy healing work? you ask. Just like your car radio, which transmits information over hundreds of miles through waves you cannot see, an energetic healer tunes into your energetic body and receives information. I specialize in clients whose lives are disrupted by dark energies—"

I scrolled to the intake form: name, email, phone number. At that point, I would have told her my birthday and home address, if I thought it would help. The website said all requests for spirit removal would receive a response within two business days. Victor and Astrid returned Saturday around noon. It was Wednesday morning. This could work, I thought as the video played on, too crazed to pay much attention. Nadia was talking about eagle vision—"it's about soaring above the chaos, having a clear perspective; ever notice how the eagle has four talons on each foot, which connects us to the four elements, the four corners of the earth, the four seasons, the transformation of four"—when Nathan appeared on the threshold.

"Knock knock, I just wanna come in. What're you doing?"

I closed the laptop. "Trying to solve the mystery of the bloated yogurt," I said, abruptly pleased with the lie. It sounded like a bad Nancy Drew. "Yesterday we swabbed the plant. Equipment, loading zone, loading dock, hallways. Now we're waiting for lab results."

He settled into the chair opposite, hands gripping the armrests.

"Becca told me. She got in the door with me."

"In the same compartment? That sounds unpleasant."

"She was going to Starbucks. It was fun. Her hair is black and blond and striped like a skunk. And she smells good. I think she's pretty! Do you think she's pretty?"

"I never make remarks about employees' appearances for fear of sexual harassment issues. I try not to even *see* their bodies or faces." Actually, I'd noted how frequently Becca's hair changed color. "Did she say anything odd or inappropriate?"

"She told me Gotcha Matcha! tastes like seaweed and chalk."

"I'm bored." He wandered the room, rapping the walls, flicking the blinds, pulling the credenza drawers in and out. "Can I watch a movie on your laptop?"

"What a good idea!" I said, remembering Hazel had slept through *3 Ninjas* at school. But when we opened my Netflix, every movie seemed destined to activate her. *Red Dog. Angel Dog. Hachi: A Dog's Tale.* Of course, I was only seeing those movies because of what I'd watched before, but suddenly I had a better idea. We could bore the shit out of her. I shut down Netflix and fixed the browser to a live bird cam.

"Omar showed me this, hoping I'd find mediated nature calming. I think you'll like it."

Six tube feeders swaying in the wind. Off-screen: faint cheeping.

"But there's nothing to see," Nathan said.

"You have to be patient."

"Is there a highlight reel on YouTube?"

"Highlights suck, Nathan. You want the long, immersive experience of watching snow fall on feeders. The unpredictable pleasure of seeing a bird alight."

Nah, he said, but he might like a vulture live cam. Once he saw a YouTube video of a vulture attacking a mountain goat. Had I ever seen the video of a toucan pecking a parrot to death? Or a heron pulling a baby bunny out of a hole and swallowing it in one bite? Or a pygmy owl plucking a squirrel out of a tree and eating its innards like spaghetti?

"Does every story have to have a grisly end? Watch the peaceful backyard birds! I need to do my email."

"I'm hungry," he said after five minutes. "Are there any flavors other than Gotcha Matcha! in the break room?"

"Go check. Spoons are in a jar on the counter," I said as he trotted out.

Sighing, I turned back to Nadia Vizcarra Lerkins. All requests for spirit removal would receive a response within two business days. The eagle flew effortlessly above the storm, she said, not even beating its wings, etc. Cut to Nadia in the same brown smock and cape, this time seated by a swift-flowing river. Were those real fish leaping in the waves, or was the scenery fake? I'd barely heard a word she said when, from the outer office, I heard a burst of laughter.

In the suite, the entire staff had gathered in front of the cow art, where Nathan stood, hands in pockets, lecturing like he was a docent.

"And maybe you've had a chance to see a full-grown bullock? Those cows can weigh one or two thousand pounds. But the little nippers run around the outside, keeping the cows bunched up in the field, or they chase them into a corner. If you grip the bull in the tender part just above the hoof, you can keep running and swerving, and not even get kicked. Of course, it's noisy! And dusty! And smelly! But nobody—"

"What's going on?" I demanded.

The staff turned, faces enlivened.

"—nobody herds like corgis," Nathan finished. "Even if collies *do* have longer legs!"

I stared with some intensity. His hair was mussed, and his pupils were dilated, but other than that he looked normal.

"Nathan was just telling us how corgis herd cattle," Sylvia explained.

"Since 800 AD," Bill said. "I had no idea corgis went back that far."

"Agile little dogs," Pearl said. "Brave and tenacious!"

"And supercute!" Becca shook the ice in her pink drink.

"It's sad," Sylvia murmured, "how farmers drive the cows with tractors now."

"Nathan!" I sharped. "I thought you went to get a snack."

He spun around from the cow art and blinked. "I guess . . . I got lost."

I bit my tongue and tried to bore into his brain telepathically. Becca said, "It's a weird-shaped office. Want me to show you where the snacks are?"

"Come by my desk and I'll show you my candy drawer."

"How come you never show *us* your candy drawer?" Bill asked Sylvia, and everybody laughed but me.

I took Nathan by the hand. "No candy. Any minute those swabs are going to come back, and I know we all have lots to do. Please don't be bothering people," I told Nathan in a low tone.

"Ah, it was a pleasant diversion!" Doug raised his hands together and everyone applauded. "Good presentation, great factoids!" Bill added, and I was floored. Nobody ever clapped when I gave PowerPoints. The staff trailed back to their desks, and I shunted Nathan into my office and closed the door.

"I don't know what you were doing out there, but I don't like it. Little nippers? Herding since 800 AD? She's filling your brain with corgi propaganda."

"Corgi what?"

"It's the thin end of the wedge. Don't let her speak for you, all right?"

"It was just a cow and dog story. People liked it."

People just like having a chance to goof off from work. But I refrained from saying that. I didn't want to hurt his feelings; I only wanted him to understand the danger.

"You have to tell your own stories. Be your *own* person. Don't ever let anyone speak for you."

"Then why'd you speak for me when we first got here? That lady at the front desk asked what grade I was in, and you said—" He pursed his lips like he was eating something sour. " 'First grade, he goes to Rawlings Elementary. Though we're looking at Alembic Academy, tee hee.' "

"I did *not* say 'tee hee.' Anyway that's different. I was introducing you to Pearl. Don't get saucy. If you can't keep Hazel's conversation out of your mouth, you can stay in here until five and watch the bird cam."

"No fair! That's so boring."

He lay on the carpet with the laptop and didn't speak to me for the next hour, and only then because two White-Breasted Nuthatches crowded a Black-Capped Chickadee on the feeder. Time passed. We were not happy. For lunch, we ate hummus and crackers I fetched from the break room. After eating he dozed on the floor. He was still dozing at two p.m. when the labs came back. Fifty of one hundred and twenty-five swabs tested positive for *Listeria monocytogenes*.

"Oh no!"

"What's the matter?" he asked muzzily.

I sat still, my eyes fixed on the numbers, numbers that felt like a slap in the face, when your face is on the Jumbotron. Unless they were only a chess move, an offensive strategy.

"Nathan, could Hazel have messed with the lab results?"

"What're you talking about?" Sleepily he rubbed his face.

"If she can spy on Omar and Peter, she can manipulate the labs, right? I don't trust it. It's a trick. I don't trust it at all! Stay here. I'll be right back."

"Did you see the lab reports?" Doug said when I bounced in.

"Yes. But swab again."

"Why?"

"Because I have a hunch those fifty are false positives."

Doug colored, knit his brows, squeezed his purple stress ball, and said that might endanger lives. Of course, he's going to say that, I thought. What did he understand about the powers of darkness? He thought ghosts were hallucinations from fungal spores.

"You don't get it, Rose. If we swab everything again, we have to wait another twenty-four hours to take action."

"Action's exactly what she's trying to provoke. She pushes me into a costly recall, and laughs while I lose my family *and* my assets."

Doug looked confused. "Who? Did you talk to a biochemist? I'd like to be looped in."

Pearl poked her head into the office. She just got off the phone, she said, with Weiss Memorial Hospital. Bad news. "They won't release the patient's name. But somebody ate Gotcha Matcha! and was admitted with acute gastrointestinal distress. I can call back in an hour and get a status check."

"They specifically said Gotcha Matcha!?" I asked Pearl.

Doug covered his face with his hands.

"Halt production," I said. "Commit to a voluntary recall."

Chapter 23

A recall is a delicate business. You have to own up to the problem but also reassure customers. Could I say the yeast in yogurt usually outcompetes any harmful bacteria? Could I emphasize that other Cultured Cow products were not a part of this recall? Had we pulled the product on Tuesday when Doug suggested, I could have said, No injuries or illnesses have been reported to date, and what a lovely sentence that would have been! Now the best I could say as I crafted the press release was "The Cultured Cow identified the issue after receiving a consumer complaint and has elected to immediately remove all Gotcha Matcha! from retail shelves. Although the problem is not widespread, our first priority has always been and will always be the health and well-being of our consumers."

Nathan asked why my forehead was creased.

"I'm trying to squash *Listeria* hysteria."

"What's *Listeria*?"

"An infection you get from eating food that has *Listeria monocytogenes.*"

"Bad bacteria," Doug clarified as he swooped in and dropped some paperwork on my desk. "Here's the recall insurance you'll be glad to know I *did* renew." (I'd dragged my heels about it.) "Call Mona Shea with questions."

The bird feeders were empty again, swaying in the wind. Nathan rolled onto his back and gazed at the ceiling. "Hazel says there's no such thing as good bacteria or bad bacteria. Just badly loved bacteria."

"Tell that dumb dog *Listeria is* bad. Especially if people are old or frail or pregnant."

"Why do you hate her so much, Aunt Rose?"

"I'm writing the press release. I don't have time to discuss it."

"Mary said mean things about her, but they aren't true. *You* know. You kept Walter even though people don't like him."

Plenty of people like Walter, I said. Didn't Nathan realize? Children beg to pet him. The vet gives him treats. The groomer calls him Black Bean Burrito. Omar happily looked after him, without pay, when I booked a six-day vegan tour of Paris.

The uplifting memory of that trip sunk under a wave of shame. Why had I said those shitty things to Omar? For the same reason, I supposed, one ever says anything brash. I was stretched to my limit, and he'd riled me up by saying

I talk too much. How could I *not* feel stung, especially after learning Victor and Astrid called me Aunt Rant?

"I'll look after Walter sometime," Nathan promised. "Remember when he was a puppy and sat on the dishwasher? Mommy said it was gross you let him lick the plates."

"The dishes always went through a hot cycle."

"I know. But Mommy said they were people plates and he was a bad dog."

Mommy's neurotic. "I have to write this press release, Nathan."

"Good dog, bad dog. Hazel says nobody knows!"

"She's a moral relativist now? I'm glad to win the dishwasher argument. But anyone equipped with some life experience is clear on the difference between a good and a bad dog, just as they're clear on what makes a good or bad person."

I returned to the press release. Too deferential? Too confident? If the hospital patient croaked, in retrospect would it appear heartless?

"What's a good person?" pursued Nathan.

"*You* know." In a fit of pique, I deleted the whole paragraph. "Someone who is honest, loyal, trustworthy, fair. Someone who tries to help others."

"How do you know Hazel isn't helping?"

"I guess I don't." The clouds gathered over me, the moon concealed her light, the vapors rose, quivering round my head (figuratively speaking; we were still in my office, under the fluorescents). "Maybe she *could* help us." I rolled my chair back from the desk.

"Really?"

"She knows the Bennett kid is getting an appendectomy. Maybe she can use her oracular powers and tell me if—if—"

"Aunt Rose! You want to talk to Hazel?"

"Not talk exactly, but I mean— Oops!" I rolled to the left and banged my shin on the file cabinet. "This recall business is difficult to know how to spin. I'm open—if you want to repeat anything she has to say, regarding corporate strategy . . . Anything that would help me know how far out I need to go in terms of defense—"

Nathan sprung to his feet and did a jerky little dance—the kind of dance you do when you're too young to know that it is possible to fail at dance—and flung himself at my feet. My insides liquified: Was I about to do business with a dark entity?

"Knock knock!" Cheeks flushed; delighted.

"Who's there?"

"Ego."

"Ego who?"

"Ego up the mountain and not come down."

It meant nothing to me.

"Is that it? I was hoping for something with practical applications."

Nathan rolled around on his back, like Walter rolling in a stinky patch of grass. My gaze drifted back to my computer.

A while later he asked, "Is the person who ate the yogurt dead now? Are they going to be dead? Do you think they're okay with being dead?"

"I don't know. I was hoping Hazel could tell me all that."

But Hazel, it seemed, couldn't be worked.

No more eBay auctions. No more YouTube surfing. On my desk was a long list of action items: file with the Department of Agriculture, hire a food lab, plan for a factory reset, dispose of the yogurt. Two hours on the phone with our lawyer and a microbiology consultant.

We still didn't know how the *Listeria* had got in, but since multiple vendors reported bloat, and we had those swabs, I conceded the problem was on our end—my end?—our end. Anyway I hefted to the side my suspicions about Hazel.

Instead I asked, How could we fix it? Refrigeration? Trucks? Maybe we needed regular third-party testing for bacteria and a hold-test-release program.

"If the FDA chooses to audit the recall—"

"I'm gathering information," Doug said. "We've sent questionnaires to everyone along the distribution chain. The FDA coordinator says—"

"You've been in touch with the FDA?"

"Yesterday. Under the circumstances, it seemed wise."

"Good work. High level of organization. I mean, what am I saying? Thanks," I croaked.

Because I had assailed and obstructed him at every turn, Doug's expression brightened only a small degree, like after a brownout.

The rest of the day, I kept my door open. Pearl kept me abreast of the consumer and media calls. Bill and Sylvia traipsed in and out, sharing updates on various vendors. We were a little company and had to hustle. McDonald's could have rat shit in their salads, I told Nathan, and it wouldn't affect their market share, but we only had the three flavors (Gotcha Matcha!, Vanilla Has Bean, and Coco Loco), so we needed to reassure our customers. The minute I said Coco Loco, Nathan shouted, Loco! Loco! and ran around, knocking over wastepaper baskets. But most of the time he watched the bird cam, whispered knock-knock jokes, or sat at Becca's feet, making a garland out of paper clips. At six thirty, we were still hunkered down. No way would we be home in time to make Vegan Lasagna with Tofu Ricotta. I took my intern's suggestion and ordered dinner from a Mexican chain, which came in a ridiculous number of plastic containers, with a stack of paper napkins as fat as a dictionary. I laid it all out on the conference table and the staff drifted in, excited by the smell. Nathan scarfed two chimichanga plates, spilling rice and salsa all over the office carpet, and no one said anything. People were nice to him.

"That was fun!" Nathan said when, at last, I locked the outer office door and (after a final, giddy turn through the revolving door) we plunged into the parking lot. Becca, drifting past in white hat and blue shearling coat, gave Nathan's head a parting pat, which he received with a satisfied shiver. I hurried us into the car.

"Aunt Rose," Nathan said as I steered sharply toward the street. "Do you still want to sell the company?"

"Yes, but if the business tanks, I won't be able to sell it. Not for much, anyway."

"But don't you think it was fun today, everybody working and helping?"

I laughed drily. "This isn't the part where I suddenly decide I love yogurt and want to save the company. I want to sell The Cow at a profit and then, for the sake of ecological justice, let the next owner run it into the ground. I think maybe you watch too much television."

We drove the rest of the way in silence.

Chapter 24

The remainder of that evening was spent walking Walter (slightly distraught at having been left alone so long) and convincing Nathan (highly energized by being part of "The Cultured Cow team") that it was advisable to go to bed, despite his announcement that he had achieved a second wind. Did I want to play Boggle? Did I want to do a puzzle? Did I want to play UNO? I did not, but cheerlessly sagged on the sofa while he tug-of-warred with Walter until close to ten o'clock. Then I shooed him off to the bathroom.

From the hallway, I heard him mucking around, further delaying bedtime. He turned the water on and off, flushed the toilet, dropped in the sink what sounded like an andiron, played briefly with my hairdryer—and the whole time he was gabbling away. "Who's there?" he shrieked. "Shirley who?" A rash of giggles at the punch-line, which obviously I missed. That's fine, I thought, permissive because exhausted. Let him unleash her in the privacy of the bathroom; tomorrow Nadia Vizcarra Lerkins will call back, and we'll flush her out!

Nathan emerged and the door almost smacked me in the face.

"What are you doing there?"

"Coming to see if you flossed."

He nodded, yawning widely enough for me to inspect his molars, and just as I was gearing up for a shred or two more of conversation, he gave me a floppy high five.

"I guess I *am* tired. Or maybe it's just the chimichangas hitting me."

He scuffled off to the Wevet room. I stood there, bereft.

Out of habit I picked up my phone to call Omar, then remembered. *Oh.* So I turned to Doug D'Andrea's dairy disposal checklist. Walter bulldozed into the living room, barking, jowls dripping from a recent drink, and ploughed into my lap. He kept wagging and shoving me, unable to distinguish my push from play. I had to stand up and screech before he finally quit and slunk off. After dropping to the floor, he glared. I glared back. Was the whole world dissatisfied with me?

Why had I yelled at Omar and needled him about the dead diver? It wasn't *his* fault she'd had an aneurysm. It was true—and somewhat ridiculous—he had a land line, but he still had customers. I'd just needed to give him a poke.

I crept into Nathan's room and swiped three of his melatonin, then lay in my Spanish colonial queen—serpentine pilasters, turned bun feet—but the most unpleasant parts of the day floated into my mind, like vegetable peels in a sink of dirty dishwater.

Omar was my best friend—the only person in my life whom I found satisfying in all emotional weathers and lights. Too bad I'd mentioned all the gifts I'd given him—especially that Gordon Martz vase—because now it might seem like I was keeping count. Was I keeping count? I pulled the blanket up to my chin and curled my legs around Walter, whose paws were wet from stepping in his water dish. That awful Punta Tosca thing! I had gladly paid Omar's legal fees and never expected him to pay me back. I'd made it sound like I regretted the expense, but only because he'd made my family sound like a pathetic soap opera. Oh yeah, and if he was the Ear, what was I? The Mouth? Maybe if he hadn't been all broody about his secret boyfriends, I wouldn't even have exploded.

Omar knows me, I kept saying to myself. He knows I can be a hothead. Maybe he wasn't even mad, just laughing because I'd had another one of my outbursts. "Rose's thorns," he called them once.

I snatched my phone off the nightstand to see if there was anything—a cautious hello or a heart emoticon; maybe a silly GIF.

Nothing. Our last exchange was Sunday night when I'd seen the corgi. I'd said, "Something weird happened," and he'd said, "I'm out to dinner. Catch up later?"

Then I'd texted him. Fourteen times. How stupid! I got up and went to the bathroom. Walter jumped off the bed and padded after me. As I tried to pee, I stared at the tiled floor, at Nathan's toothbrush, at the thick Turkish towels, bought for Nathan's visit, hanging on the rail. Walter followed me to the living room, where the window frames were edged with snow. I couldn't see the moon. And it was snowing again—tiny flakes, but likely to stick. How stupid, how stupid! When I texted Omar fourteen times, I hadn't *known* he'd been on a date. But I might have remembered I'd given him the symphony tickets for that night. Or asked about his evening the next morning when I called from Rawlings. And today I shouldn't have been so impatient when he was trying to take another call. Shame rippled over me like caramel on a crappy McDonald's sundae.

The more I thought about it, the worse I felt.

Chapter 25

Early the next morning, while I walked Walter, the sky dumped freezing rain. The wind blew straight in my face. It seemed like a fair penalty. Once home, I roused Nathan, gave him a large breakfast, and packed the BMW with books and toys and snacks. Yesterday I'd arranged for us to drive downstate to the plant, where I would personally supervise the destruction of thousands of pounds of yogurt. But there was no joy in it.

On the way out of town, we stopped at the dive shop, which wouldn't open until ten, and I slid an envelope under the front door.

"That was a note for Omar," I explained as I slipped back into the car.

"Why didn't you just text him?"

"I took a tip from your principal, Dr. Bossy or whatever his name is."

"Ha ha. You made a joke!" Nathan tried to wipe the condensation off the windscreen, but the fog clung to the outside. "Dr. Abbassi *is* kind of bossy."

"A handwritten apology," I elaborated. "I'm sure Omar would rather get a handwritten note than a text or yet another email in that black hole of his inbox."

"What're you apologizing for?"

"It's complicated."

"When am I going to write *my* apologies?"

"After we destroy the yogurt."

"Are you crying?" he asked, peering suspiciously at my face.

"No. My eyes are watering from the cold."

"Turn up the heater," he advised and did it himself. Then he sprung open the glove compartment, shut it. Opened it. Shut it. Opened it.

"Enough fiddling. Want to hear about the environmental niceties of dairy waste disposal?"

"Not really."

"Want to hear about a rival food processing company that got fined for dumping dairy waste directly into the sewer system through floor drains and sewer inlets?"

"No."

Fine then. I could keep my musings to myself. I didn't need to say everything I thought. I would be a new, more modulated person; I would focus on the road. Or maybe we could play license plate games.

"You can't really *see* the license plates," Nathan pointed out.

"They should give people tickets for not removing the snow." I turned on the radio just as WFMT began playing Bach Cello Suite No. 1. Oblivious to the haunting melody, Nathan began to count out loud.

"Four . . . five . . . six . . ."

"What are you counting?"

"All the cars passing us."

"Seven . . . eight—"

"Okay, I get your point."

"Aunt Rose."

"Yes."

"Why are you driving like a snail?"

"It's winter, Nathan."

"But the highway's ploughed. Nine! Don't you see how everyone else is—why don't you switch lanes?"

Who was hectoring me, him or the corgi? Either way I didn't like it.

"I'm staying in the slow lane, no matter what you say. I'm in charge."

"Be the alpha."

I scanned his face for sarcasm. No trace. Driving on, I let my thoughts loop back to Omar. Writing and delivering the apology, I'd felt a surge of relief, maybe even confidence. I really did owe him an apology. But now there was nothing to do but fill time and feel bad. When would Omar read my letter? How soon would he forgive me? How long would I have to sit in this puddle, cringing with shame?

"Can I change the station?"

No, he could not. Bach Cello Suite No. 1, I explained, was historically important in that it showed the cello could be a solo instrument. Listen carefully, and he'd realize it's one instrument achieving the effect of three or four contrapuntal voices. He wasn't in school today, but he could still learn.

"I don't want to learn what you know."

"Oh yeah?"

"I want to learn my own stuff."

"What kind of 'stuff'?"

"Never mind." And he twitched the dial, shoving Bach off the airwaves, replacing a sonorous cello with two garrulous DJs on 103.5 KISS-FM.

Repelled by their chatter, I swiped the dial, but we only received the nerve-blasting static roar between stations. "Fix that please," I said, both hands on the wheel. He knew what I meant, but whizzed over to a Spanish-language station and then, when I said retune, landed on a loud and brutishly optimistic hair transplant commercial, prompting me to slap his hand and swipe the dial myself. Was he taunting me? *She* was taunting me! The highway stretching whitely before us, I wrestled him for the dial, achieving a measure or two of Bach's courante before he struck back, swinging to a classic rock station playing "We Built This City," the sonic equivalent of Dorothy picking up a bucket of water in *The Wizard of Oz* and wetting the witch from head to foot. I gave a loud cry ("Look what you've done! I'm melting! Melting!") and unconsciously pressed the gas. "I like this song!" he shrieked. In the so-called slow lane, going sixty miles an hour, we seemed bound—almost spiritually appointed—to hit a sheet of ice. Time slowed. The car began to spin. The deficiencies of Nathan's chosen song unfurled before me with the clarity of a sacred scroll, and yet even as I remarked on its stupid synthesizers and shoddy, tedious lyrics, I was capaciously able to wonder: Would we smash another car, crash through the guard rail, roll into the ditch, fly through the windshield, get crushed against the door? Would we die on this highway? The car spun ten or eleven times. Behind us cars honked and swerved. My internal organs did not pucker in terror. Some part of me found it pleasurable to be, at last, out of control.

Chapter 26

In a suburb three miles west of where our car came to
a stop on the highway, on a strip of road that featured
an abandoned movie theatre, a discount shoe store, and a
cemetery bordered by a six-foot-high metal fence capped
with snow, there stood a hospital, founded in affiliation
with the Evangelical Lutheran Church and rooted in the
belief that all persons are created in the image of God, a
hospital that had not in the past five years received higher
than a two-star Yelp review.

"My neck hurts," Nathan whined.

"Keep talking to me," I said, legs shaking as I navigated us to the ER.

The waiting room was small and hot and smelled of
disinfectant. A cagey nurse glanced at Nathan and told us
to hold on to the clipboard. Seated in a corner, I worked
on my agitation as if it were bread dough. Six televisions
played six different channels. There were children and old
people and a disheveled woman loudly complaining she
was bleeding from her anus. After two hours, the street

doors slid open, and a man bounded past the security guard wearing sweatpants and a fisherman's sweater.

"There you are!" cried Omar.

"Where's your coat?"

Sweet human! From the dive shop (I assumed) he'd rushed to us, and as soon as he verified our general safety, he hurried across the waiting room and bought candy and pretzels from vending machines I hadn't known existed and, like a retriever dropping grouse, deposited them on Nathan's lap. He was competent, energetic, aware. I teemed with gratitude and inwardly noted the power of an apology.

"This hospital is run by Neanderthals," I said when he inquired how soon we might be seen. "So who knows? That triage nurse—she's like a lizard sleeping on a rock."

A Snickers wrapper drifted onto my thigh.

"How bad is the pain?"

"Not bad really." I touched my forehead. "But Nathan—"

"I got slammed against the door," Nathan said cheerfully.

"Your whole body?"

"No, just my head. My neck. But before, it was actually *fun*, Omar! We did donuts!"

"It was not fun," I lied. "Nor will it be fun if you have whiplash."

"Or a concussion," Omar said.

"I hadn't thought of that."

"You're lucky she didn't kill somebody."

"She?" Nathan said. "You mean Hazel? You think *she* did it?"

Omar didn't answer, but sat stiff-legged, expelling breath through his nostrils, like a horse.

Nathan smiled. "Knock knock!"

Omar pressed his lips together. Not playing.

"Who's there?"

"Leash."

"Leash who?"

"Leash we didn't kill ourselves!"

He broke up laughing, and I laughed a little, too.

Omar looked at us coolly. "I'm glad you're both taking this seriously."

Maybe I was laughing out of shock? I'd hit my head, I explained. But honestly, I was so grateful he'd accepted my apology and come.

"What apology?" Omar said blankly.

"Didn't you get my letter? I put it under your door."

"At my house?"

"No, the dive shop."

"Frogman is closed on Thursdays. It's always closed on Thursdays."

"Why would it be closed on Thursdays?"

"I stay open all weekend, so I'm closed on Wednesdays and Thursdays."

"Midweek you close? Geez, Omar, no wonder revenues are down."

He shook his head, eyes closed.

"I'm just saying: If you'd gone to work like a normal person, you would've found it."

"Found *what*?"

"The apology I put under the dive shop door."

"Oh my god. You *wrote* it?"

"What?"

"Is it subject to terms and conditions?"

I stared.

"Why didn't you just call me if you had something to say?"

"That's what I said," Nathan said, pitching pretzels into his mouth.

"I handwrote it. To be gracious. And now—now I'm confused. I was thinking you came because you read it."

"I came because you texted me 'we had a car accident and we're in the emergency room!!!' Three exclamation points. You pinned your location."

"I was in shock," I whispered.

No answer.

"NATHAN CUTLER," bawled a nurse in pink scrubs.

We stood up and headed her way, Omar spitting into my ear.

"I've been trying to help, and all you do is interrupt and yell. I try to help and you get *mean*. You know nothing about quarry diving, by the way."

"I realize that now." We hurried through a set of pneumatic doors and through a narrow hallway lined with carts and equipment. "I did apologize. The timing's unfortunate, but you'll see—I apologized for being a really bad listener."

"When?" Omar said.

"This morning."

"No, I mean when do you think you were—"

"Sunday. Tuesday. Okay, lots of times! Can't you just read it?"

"Can't you just say it?"

We reached a tiny room without a door. No one was in it.

"Wait here," the nurse said, cinching a plastic curtain, and went away. Nathan scrambled onto the exam table, shouting "Hi-yah!" He jiggled his legs, ripped the crepe paper on the table, drummed the wall with both hands. Omar sighed, lowering himself into the only chair.

"Is this even an emergency?" he said.

Chapter 27

The doctor sidled in, a compact woman in her sixties. White coat. Red sneakers. Nametag: Dr. Chau.

"Ho, ho, ho," she said with more fatigue than joy. "You're not here for that eye, are you?"

No, Nathan said proudly, he got the black eye Tuesday at school. But today we did a bunch of donuts on the highway and he got thrown against the door. We should've kept driving to throw away the bloated yogurt, but *she* said (he pointed a grubby finger at me) we had to stop because maybe he broke his neck.

"You didn't break your neck. Where does it hurt?"

The moment the doctor moved closer, I had to steady my breath. Nathan submitted easily to her examination ("Does this hurt? What about this? Can you move ear to shoulder? Chin to shoulder?"), but I regretted that, rather than just give Nathan a Tylenol, I'd transferred control to a stranger. What if she detected the underlying problem? What if she thought Nathan was mentally ill, or I was mentally ill and unable to care for him? I longed for Nadia Vizcarra Lerkins and her promise of non-judgmental care. I must extract us from this weird Lutheran hospital, I thought, just as Dr. Chau dropped her hands and announced:

"You're fine."

"He's fine?"

"Yes, just a little sore, Mom."

"I'm not his mom," I said awkwardly. "I'm his aunt."

"Well, whoever you are, he's a little sore, but he'll be fine in a few days. It's not an emergency," she added, in case I'd failed to realize I was wasting her time.

"I told her I didn't need a doctor!" Still on the exam table, Nathan scooted closer to Dr. Chau. "Aunt Rose likes to worry. It's like a hobby."

Ha ha, I said, and briskly reminded the room Nathan had hit his head.

"Any headache? Dizziness? Nausea? Pupils aren't dilated. Did you vomit after the car accident? No. Cut back on physical activities, no screens for a few days, sleep if you're tired. You'll be fine."

"I knew it!" Nathan said. "Though an X-ray would have been fun."

"Don't worry so much, Aunt. But call his pediatrician if he develops symptoms or passes out."

Nathan touched the doctor's sleeve. "Aunt Rose worries a lot. She worries about Daddy and dairy products and even my dog—"

"What kind of dog do you have?"

"She's a corgi."

The doctor laughed with delight. "I love corgis! They don't have tails and their butts look like loaves of bread."

"*Yes! Yes!*" Nathan laughed maniacally. "Hazel's butt was like that before she was an inside dog."

No question about "inside" dogs. Instead Dr. Chau told him about her chihuahuas—one of whom had only three teeth. "And he uses them to bite people's ankles! He's awful! He's an awful dog! But you know what? Everyone loves Shorties. I'll show you." She took out her phone and flashed a picture. Bulging eyes. Apple head. Not my type at all—actually quite hideous—but Omar promptly said "Aww!" in a practiced way and Nathan did a whole-body shiver and began to bark as if Shorties were the devil's spawn.

"Yep, that's Shorties!" Dr. Chau said, as if Nathan's response were not entirely bizarre.

Bark. Bark bark bark. Lassie-like intensity, a someone's-in-danger bark.

"Ha ha ha! And Shorties says ruff, ruff ruff ruff. Actually," Dr. Chau said, "he'd probably say grrrrrrr."

Omar and I stood, stiff with disbelief, as Dr. Chau neglected the woman in the waiting room bleeding from her anus so she and Nathan could laugh and bark at each other. "Here's Shorties in a Bears shirt." She scrolled through her phone. "Here's my other boo-boo face. Her name is Taco. Do you like tacos? . . . Oh, hahaha, here's Shorties in a bow tie . . . Taco in her bed . . . Taco under

179

my desk . . . Taco being Taco . . . Know what she's afraid of? The blender, the vacuum cleaner, shiny floors . . ."

"Do you think you could give me an X-ray?" Nathan asked.

Dr. Chau smiled indulgently. They'd made a canine connection. "I bet you've never seen a real X-ray, just those clunky things in the airport."

Nathan nodded, tilted his head. Puppy-dog eyes.

"All right," Dr. Chau said, as if radiation were every American boy's birthright. "Let's rule out a herniated disc."

"Hooray!" Nathan said.

Dr. Chau whisked Nathan off to another room, and Omar and I were shot, like pinballs, back to the hall.

Chapter 28

"Should I have gone with him?" I asked when we were seated.

"Frankly," Omar muttered, "I feel safer when he's with other people."

"Even if he has a corgi in him, he's a minor."

"This is good. We need to talk privately. Tell me about the accident."

"I was driving and Nathan reached for the radio."

"From the back seat? How could he?"

"He was in the front seat."

"Isn't that illegal?"

"But he was belted. When I was a kid, I rode in the front seat. Anyway I was driving way too fast—"

"Highly unlikely. I've driven with you."

"And it was icy. We started squabbling over the radio. I don't know why, but I wanted *my* music—"

"First she picks a fight with Tommy. Now she picks a fight with you. It's escalating. She's evil!"

I rubbed my head. "Are you sure that's what happened?"

"You're the most cautious driver in Illinois and she put your car into a spin. If you'd spun into oncoming traffic, you'd be in a body bag right now."

"Don't frighten me."

"Rose." He got out his phone. "The Archdiocese of Chicago has a full-time exorcist whose task is to heal afflicted people."

I scoffed, but he thumb-typed furiously and showed me a map.

"There are twelve Catholic churches within five miles of your house."

"Forget it."

"You need help."

"Not that kind of help."

"I couldn't even masturbate last night," he whispered. "The thought of a corgi watching me."

"You masturbate?"

He shook his head. "Rose. Call the priest."

"I'm Jewish!" I bellowed.

"But Nathan's not. He's *Cashew*. And the Catholic Church knows more about exorcisms than anybody."

"So I should confide in some random child molester?"

"They're not all child molesters."

"Should we look up the percentages? You know the Catholic Church has been hating on women and gay people for two thousand years. No way would I entrust

Nathan to their care." I threw back my head, then erupted into a coughing fit that sounded like I was about to expire, when in fact I was choking on my own saliva. Did I need a whack on the back? he asked, but spluttering, I refused. Together we stood and headed for the water fountain. I stopped coughing, stooped over to drink, and spilled cold water all over my shirt. Omar shook his head.

"Would you be willing to call a rabbi?"

"I'd rather play Tzeitel in *Fiddler on the Roof*!"

The X-ray took almost an hour so we got lost in our phones. I texted Doug I was no longer en route to destroy the yogurt; checked my spam folder for messages from Nadia; ignored Victor's two voicemails and a text from Astrid re: an automated message from Rawlings re: Nathan's absences. Omar played *Fruit Ninja* until I nudged him.

"Do you think Victor and Astrid will buy it if I say I kept Nathan home with strep?"

"Strep requires antibiotics. Say sore throat and fever. And please, please, please consider the exorcist rather than go it alone."

"I'm trying to go it with *you*."

"I don't want to be part of it anymore!" He waved his hands, aggrieved and suddenly misty. "It's too big and scary. Way over our heads. Not to mention the fact that I was sexually violated. I think I'm going to go." He nodded, shook his head, made as if to stand up. "My therapist says I'm an overgiver."

"Nathan's parents!" bawled the nurse.

Stunned, we stared at each other.

"Oh all right," Omar sighed, and we trailed back into the exam room where Dr. Chau waited alone.

"Nothing's wrong with his neck. He just needs to rest it. But what a genius with a knock-knock joke! We laughed ourselves silly. Laughter—that's the real cure for whatever ails you."

"Where is he?" I said flatly.

"Cervical orthosis. The PA is fitting him. Just a little extra support."

The curtain rasped and Nathan minced in, blushing and smiling, neck encased in a six-inch belt of blue foam rubber.

"This relieves spinal pressure!" Dr. Chau adjusted the collar further, with tenderness. "Because it makes it hard to move, you won't ever hurt yourself, even if you go chasing a corgi."

She and Nathan gazed at each other, like lovers in a romantic movie; the cold furniture, the plastic curtain, the other humans, it all fell away.

"When can he take it off?" I asked.

She winked. "Whenever he feels better."

She led our cortege through the corridor, back to the waiting room, past the triage desk, and all the way to the lobby doors, where the security guard seemed surprised to see her.

Chapter 29

SAT: Pan-fried Tempeh and String Beans

SUN: ~~Sweet N Spicy Bean Cakes with Cashew~~ *peanut butter*
~~Cream Dressing. Kale, Apple, Walnut Salad.~~ *on crackers*

MON: Lentil Loaf, Braised Carrots, Mashed Potatoes,
Greens

TUES: ~~Roasted Buttercup Squash Cups with~~ *Thai carryout*
~~Apple Slaw~~

WED: ~~Vegan Lasagna with Tofu Ricotta~~ *Mexican delivery*

THURS: Millet Red Bean Chili ~~and Pumpkin Spice~~
~~Quick Bread~~

FRI: Armenian Stuffed Eggplant, Tabbouli, and Hummus

The ER was a signal event for Nathan. He'd never been injured before, and now he had a story to tell. He told it many times, like the Ancient Mariner.

I had to lie on a table. And they put a shield on me so I wouldn't get poisoned. And then this other lady moved the X-ray machine over my neck, and Dr. Chau showed me the image, and it wasn't just my neck but my *tonsils*, and my *trachea*, and I had to hold my breath the whole time so the image wouldn't get blurry, and Dr. Chau laughed at my jokes and told me her daughter has a dog named Butters . . .

When I got tired of hearing it, he told it to Walter.

For dinner I made Millet Lentil Chili but skipped the Pumpkin Spice Quick Bread. As Nathan ate, dropping beans and millet all over the tablecloth, he mentioned he *knew* we wouldn't be hurt when the car started spinning because Hazel told him so. "She was yapping at you while we were doing donuts?" No, she hadn't yapped. He'd just felt it. Hazel watching over us.

"She's a guardian angel now?" I sneered and stood up roughly, wishing I could clear his romantic notions as easily as our plates.

No surprise, he went off to the Wevet room early, a full hour before his bedtime. Unhappily I imagined Hazel filling Nathan's brain with her corgi fumes, the two of them basking in private joys.

On Friday morning things started dripping. Snow dripped. Regret dripped. Icicles crashed suddenly onto the pavement. The temperature was thirty-two degrees, and when Walter went out into the backyard, his paws soaked in muddy puddles.

It was two business days after I'd emailed Nadia Vizcarra Lerkins. Any moment she might call, and then it would be goodbye Hazel. I hoped.

When was the last time I felt something as fragile and filamentary as hope?

I woke Nathan by clapping my hands loudly. He sat up, startled.

"Is it time to go to The Cow?"

"No! The hospital patient who ate Gotcha Matcha!? They're safe! They're alive! I just got the email."

"Oh." He sunk back into bed.

"And Doug's going to dispose of the contaminated yogurt, so we don't have to go downstate to supervise. Good news!"

Nathan closed his eyes. "Nothing's good or bad. Just thinking makes it so."

He'd slept in the foam collar.

I asked, "How do you feel? Do you still have a headache?"

"I think it's gone."

"More good news," I insisted and asked what he wanted for breakfast.

No answer. I wrenched open the drapes, and the winter light fell on his face. Overnight the bruised eye had bloomed into new sick shades of purple; here and there his hair stuck up in odd fins.

I proposed he take off the collar.

"She told me to wear it," he said.

"Hazel?"

"Dr. Chau. Remember?" And then he added thoughtfully, "She was *nice*."

Nice. Because she'd laughed heartily at his jokes and made a game of the X-ray?

I too could be nice.

With a sumptuous air, I reprised my pancakes, but wanting to surprise him, I skipped the aquafaba as a binder. Only when Nathan had taken his first bite did I ask him to—

"Guess the egg replacement!"

"I dunno."

"Don't you want to try?"

"Not really."

"Does Hazel know?"

"I don't think so."

"Ask her."

"She doesn't know, Aunt Rose."

"I thought she knew everything," I said with a hollow laugh. "The answer is mashed banana."

He didn't gratify me with a reply. "When are we going to The Cow?"

"We're not." I pointed at him to wipe his mouth. "I'm taking the day off."

"But don't you have to help with the recall?"

"You need to rest your neck, and Doug agreed he could manage. You and I have bigger fish to fry."

"What are we frying?" A quaver in his voice. He knew some sorrow lurked in the wings.

"It's Hazel. She's going to leave today."

"No!" he cried and dropped his fork. His hands floated up to his face and covered his eyes, as if she could see out of them, and he wanted to protect her from my sight. "But how?"

"I hired someone to get rid of her."

Of course, he argued. Not today—he needed to write his apologies. Didn't I want him to learn to play chess? And what about the meals we'd missed, the ones in the binder? We should cook them! We should listen to more of that Mahler guy. Weren't there more numbers? When he saw I couldn't be budged, he ran to the Wevet room, threw himself across the bed, and wept.

It was the first day all week the sun had shone. When he quieted, I coaxed him into his coat and the two of us walked Walter through the melting snow, avoiding pedestrians, dogs, puddles. Water trickled off the roofs; birds cheeped; in places you could make out the grey cement of the sidewalks. Only Walter showed any glee, bounding off to a shrub where someone had flung a greasy Styrofoam clamshell. I let him lick it clean.

Back at the house, we shed our filthy boots and Nathan asked when the person was coming over to get Hazel. I don't know, I admitted. What are they going to do? he asked. I don't know. Where are they going to *put* her? I don't know. Well, how's it going to work? he asked, and I snapped, I'd know when the person called me back.

Encouraged by my inability to supply a single concrete detail, Nathan sauntered off to play.

Why had I gotten stuck on Nadia Vizcarra Lerkins? I'd lost all this time, waiting for her to call me back! For all I knew, she was never going to call. I needed a backup dark entity removal specialist. I sunk into an armchair, Googled and clicked indiscriminately on websites.

$6.29 Original Price:~~$6.92~~ (9% Off)

Dark energy, Curse, Hex or Evil Eye Identification to Banish Forever - Identify Dark Attachment and understand how it can be removed.

MY NAME IS JOSH.
MY GIFT IS CLAIRCOGNIZANCE.
PLEASE SHARE WITH ME A RECENT PICTURE.
I WILL CLEAR YOU OF PARASITES IN 15-60 MINUTES.

Dr. Anvi Vashishta is a famous author and alternative therapy practitioner. Dr. Vashishta has won the Elite Bengal Plus Size Diva beauty pageant and bagged the subtitle of Miss Beauty with Brains. Submit a check-up request today! Dark Entity Removal, Spell Casting, Magnet Therapy, DNA Healing, and Palmistry.

Who were these people? How could I tell if they were good? Why were all their websites made with the same crappy color scheme and cosmic-themed clip art?

None of them had videos like Nadia.

Still in his foam collar, Nathan approached, holding a tin box of magic markers.

"Can I have some paper?" He fixed my face with the baleful gaze of a basilisk. "I want to write my apologies."

Chapter 30

"Whose do you want to do first?" I asked as we sat together at the table. "Shingler or Tommy?"

"Tommy." But after picking a piece of paper, he sucked the end of his marker, not knowing what to write.

"Just say what you feel," I said feebly.

"I don't know what I feel."

"Dear Tommy, I'm sorry we fought in Reading Lab—"

"But I'm not sorry."

"It's a hoop you have to jump through."

"Why?"

"Life is tedious. Life is like that— Oh no," I said as he began to write. "You made your D backwards again. Don't you see—"

"This is stupid! I don't think he's sorry and I'm not sorry either. I was the alpha. You said I should be the alpha!"

"I meant with Hazel!"

"Did you?" He turned, and—definite as a picture in a frame—the black-rimmed eyes of the corgi stared back at me.

I pushed away my chair, shaken.

Tommy Bessinger glommed on to Nathan in nursery school. Their alliance was so unlikely it seemed Tommy only wanted someone weaker to push around. He had a dirty neck and a reputation for willfulness. Once I brought a rhubarb custard tart to Nathan's house, and Tommy snatched three pieces without a word. Once he broke the trunk off a wooden elephant I'd bought Nathan for Christmas. (Danish midcentury, patinated oak with articulated limbs.) Another time the boys jabbered under the slide at the park in a "top-secret" language, ignoring my bids at conversation, but this thought blurred and slipped away. Nathan wasn't writing. He pressed his marker into the paper and held it there, watching the ink blot bleed into a fuzzy-edged planet. Why had I spent so much time hating on a little kid, even if he *was* ill-mannered and clumsy? I was supposed to be the grown-up.

Dr. Chau was a grown-up. She liked chihuahuas, even though there was nothing particular to like. She gave Nathan a neck brace—just to make him feel safe.

As I sat there, squinting at my own poor character, an idea came into my head. It came with a blaze of excitement, like when you receive an unexpected gift—almost like the time I found a neighbor underselling his mother's Swedish porcelain at a garage sale.

"Nathan, let's replace Tommy's shirt."

"Instead of writing a letter?"

"No, but let's also get him a new shirt."

His bad mood blew off like steam from a kettle.

"Hooray! And then can we drop the shirt off at his house?"

"Cap that marker please. We'll see. What was it, a plaid flannel kind of thing? Let's go to Nordstrom's."

"No, Target."

"But Nordstrom's is nicer—"

"Target Target Target. That's where people get shirts."

"Fine. But we'll clean you up a little before we go out."

By now he'd left the table and was toying with the chess set, whose pieces we'd left in disarray on the floor, since Walter continually knocked them off the coffee table.

"Comb your hair," I said. "Take off the brace. Want me to put a little makeup on the black eye? I know I could mask it."

"Makeup! Aunt Rose, are you kidding?"

Chapter 31

Well acquainted with the store's layout, Nathan navigated our cart towards games, toys, sporting goods, groceries. He began to ask for things. I began to refuse, then concur, then refuse, then compromise. Time stretched like taffy. Every now and then I checked my phone, desperate for a message from Nadia.

"I'm hungry," Nathan said at the forty-five-minute mark.

"Let's get Tommy's shirt and go home."

He located a button-down (blue-and-brown plaid; Toddler 4) that I tactfully exchanged for a Husky Boy Small and dumped into the cart, which now contained, to my amazement, five random grocery items, three kinds of candy, a Nerf N-Strike Disk Shot, and a Transformers Arm Blaster.

The checkout line was long, but brutally efficient.

Expedition over, I lay on the living room floor exhausted, while Walter licked my chin. Nathan unpacked the bags and announced the Nerf toy needed batteries. Wait until after dinner, I said, unwilling to search the closet; we'll put it together then. The rest of the afternoon passed raggedly as I worked via phone and email on my yogurt problems, and Nathan mingled the Transformer with various chess pieces. My assurance that today was the end of Hazel's joyride evaporated: Where was the fucking healer? Meanwhile Becca Favorite would just keep rolling out distressingly casual Instagram posts ("Gotcha Matcha! With this recall, we gotcha covered!"). I copyedited every word she wrote until five o'clock. Then I emailed, "I'm checking out for the night," and called Omar.

"How was your day?"

"What?"

"How was your day?"

"Are you trying to be a better friend?"

"Yes," I said, already humiliated.

"I read your apology." After a pause to make me suffer, in which I did suffer, he went on. "It seemed . . . heartfelt."

"Did it?" I brightened. "That's a relief."

"You went long when you might have gone short, and short when you might have gone long. But I give it three stars, maybe two and a half."

"Is this a Yelp review?"

No, but it was possible, Omar admitted, he played a role in our "dynamic." Before he came out of the closet and his mother cut him off, she'd expected him to meet all her emotional needs.

I ducked into the Wevet room. Nathan was marching his Transformer over the comforter's mountainous terrain.

Possibly he brought old habits to even his newer relationships. Possibly . . .

When Omar concluded, I was seated deep in a low-slung leather chair, stroking Walter. I promise I heard it all. I just can't spit it back to you—it would sound like a Berkshire pig trying to speak birdsong.

"Let's both try to forget all the nasty things you said," Omar concluded. "As well as the nasty things I thought—but didn't say."

The conversation's only shadow fell a moment later, when I told him I'd contacted a Healing and Protection Specialist.

"Her name is Nadia Vizcarra Lerkins. She hasn't called back yet."

"New Age people are flaky. What's all that noise?"

"I'm giving Walter his kibble. Those are cheerful, excited barks."

"Sounds like a five-alarm fire. Why not call a priest?"

"Omar, I *told* you—" But just then my cell phone pinged.

I couldn't believe it. It was Becca Favorite—texting to ask a stupid question. What was wrong with Becca? I carped.

I'd *said* I was stopping work at five o'clock. I should have fired her the first time I caught her at her desk shopping for a luxury mattress. I should have fired her the day

SARA LEVINE

I discovered she lied about how many hours she'd actually spent at her marketing internship. She was young, entitled, and careless about details, unless the details involved her hair; why on earth, I asked Omar, didn't I fire Becca Favorite?

"Are you really asking me, or is this just one of those speeches where you offload stress?"

I bestowed Walter's bowl and there was silence—relatively speaking—as he fell on it.

"I'm really asking you," I said.

"Obviously you can fire Becca Favorite. You're the one who hired her. But you love hating her. Because if you didn't have Becca to blame every day, you'd have to look in the mirror and ask why you're so cranky."

I gasped.

Omar gained confidence.

"Becca Favorite isn't doing anything to you that you didn't unconsciously order. She's in your office because you *chose* her."

An insight bloomed like a moonflower, showy and white in my mind's dark night.

Walter finished eating and rubbed his face against the wall.

"Omar, do you mean it's like *The Wizard of Oz* when Dorothy realizes she doesn't need the wizard's help? That Dorothy had the power all along? That she only needs to click her heels? Thank you for saying that!"

"Sure." Omar sighed. "But *did* I say that?"

Chapter 32

The mind is a powerful instrument, capable of magnifying problems, masking solutions, casting dark shadows over the path that leads plainly through the forest! Nathan was never going to be an alpha dog. I saw that now. I'd asked a timid kid to turn himself into a mob boss overnight. But the bigger mistake, I thought as I removed Walter's bowl from the corner where he'd chased it, was thinking either you were an alpha or you were powerless.

Nathan wasn't powerless. He wasn't even the corgi's victim. He was her willing and adoring host.

That night, thanks to our impulse purchases at Target, dinner was a veggie hot dog, microwaved for two minutes, and a lightly toasted white bun, with a side of potato chips. The table looked so bare I added a Bitossi vase and my sterling silver candlesticks. Purely decorative. I hadn't lit a candle since Walter hit table height. "Fancy!" Nathan said.

As we took turns squirting shelf-stabilized toppings onto our hot dogs, we discussed the condiment controversy: Was ketchup acceptable or only mustard and relish? If it were a veggie dog, did the old-school Chicago rules apply? Pro forma; I barely attended my own remarks, though reflexively I took the mustard position.

Finally, I got down to business.

"You've been asking for a real dog for a long time, Nathan. Remember when you said that?"

"Hazel's real," he said promptly.

"Sort of." I tilted my head.

"She is—and anyway, now we're like the same person."

"Except she *isn't* a person."

"Don't you think of Walter as a person?"

"He's a dog."

"You bless him when he sneezes."

"Common courtesy."

"You talk to him out loud."

"I talk to *myself* out loud."

"Mommy calls him your furry, fanged baby." He raised his hot dog to his mouth and a glob of mustard fell on his neck brace.

A spike of hatred flared in my porcupine heart. I ate my chips, forgetting all concern about their carcinogenic properties.

"Walter's a total sweetheart," I said at last. "A big, shaggy heap of love. You know I adore him! But at the end of the day? He's not a person. He's a dog." In the doorway where he lay like a moat, Walter briefly lifted his head. "I think he heard that."

"Hazel talks to me," Nathan said.

"Walter talks too. A paw on my leg, a nudge of my hand. We communicate all the time."

"English, Aunt Rose."

"National Symbol Act of Canada," I said, pleased to have suddenly remembered. "I looked it up. Canadians don't care about loons. Since 1975 it's been all about the beaver. What else did Hazel get wrong, I wonder?"

He sulked. "I don't care."

"Why should you? It's literally trivia."

I got up and went to Walter, who rolled over for playtime and let me tickle his belly, milk his ears, barrel my head into his chest.

"It's just so nice to have a physical dog," I said, returning to the table. "Obviously a knock-knock joke's amusing, and it's pleasant to have her company at school. But if you didn't have Hazel, you could have a real dog who could run around. And play ball. Even roughhouse."

"Yeah, but Hazel's never gonna shed. Or get fleas. Or bite someone."

"Not with you in charge."

Surprised, he looked up from cramming potato chips.

"You're definitely more in command than I realized," I explained.

He nodded uncertainly.

"I just want to be sure you see the possibilities." He popped the last two inches of hot dog into his mouth. "I have reason to believe you're in a strong position to parlay this situation into a massive win."

I waited for him to ask, How? but he just kept chewing.

"I think you've achieved a gateway dog. You look totally blank. Your parents never said, Stay away from marijuana, that's the gateway drug to heroin and cocaine? Never mind, it was just an analogy. My point is, now's she here, you might be able to hit a harder drug. Pet-wise. Am I pitching this too high? If you release the ghost dog, you could trade up."

He squirted a pool of mustard onto his plate, dunked some potato chips, put them in his mouth. Eventually the idea formed in his mind.

"Wait. You think I could get—"

"*If* you release her."

"Oh."

"—without any help."

"I thought you hired some person to—"

"No, I need you to do it. But I know you can. She listens to you."

He blinked, flattered. I could see him doing the calculations. Sweet boy, compliant by nature; why not end all this wrangling and get something he genuinely wanted? *Trade ya.* He'd heard me do the command with Walter a hundred times, when Walter got hold of the trash, when

Walter got hold of a dead squirrel, when Walter got hold of Whippy. Nathan had only to say yes, and I'd drop my dinner, download Petfinder, write a check for a Golden Retriever, drive him to the local rescue. Whatever he wanted! But he said:

"No."

"You're never too young to learn how to negotiate. Try again."

"Huh?"

"It helps to seem detached, but if you throw out a hard no, the deal tanks. That's no fun for anyone. I'm giving you a do-over."

"They'll say no." He was thinking of his parents. "They always say no."

"That was before."

"Doesn't matter."

"And *you* said it the first day."

"What do you mean?"

"Aunt Rose, you said I'd be lucky if I got a goldfish."

"I did not."

"You did too. Why're you being so weird?"

"I'm teaching you how to negotiate, so you don't get taken advantage of in life!"

"Well, I don't want to."

Not having any silverware to toy with, I pushed away my plate. "Nathan Cutler, before she came along you were a nice boy."

"I am still a nice boy."

"I need you to be reasonable."

"I'm always reasonable." His lower lip trembled. "I'm the most reasonablest person in this family!"

"Most reasonable."

"Right!" he shouted.

"Then why are you hanging on? I get that you're lonely, but that's not a good reason."

"Are *you* lonely, Aunt Rose?"

The brazenness of the question! We were seated three feet apart, and suddenly there was the corgi, breathing biscuit-breath in my face.

"Let me talk to your parents about a real dog. I'll cite pediatric studies on the relationship between dog owner-ship and children's health. I know how to handle them, Nathan," I pleaded. "Just tell her to go."

"Aunt Rose," he sighed. Was it my imagination, or did his ears perk up, flick forward? "They don't listen to *you.*"

Chapter 33

Dear Tommy
sorry I hert your
feelings and I
riped your shert
It is rong to break
the rules. I will
be Caring
Nathan M.
Cutler

Nathan squinted at his handiwork and threw down the magic marker. He regarded the letter with a baffling measure of admiration. "Good! Now can we find the batteries? Oh!" he said as he sprang up from the table. "Remember? I have candy!"

"What is this exactly?" I said when he returned from the Wevet room, sucking on a gobstopper and cradling the Nerf N-Strike Disk Shot.

"It's an automatic skeet thrower."

Once we loaded the batteries, he hit the red power button, and it roared like a lawn mower.

"Don't launch in here! And don't launch anywhere near the dog! Or your eyes!"

"I got it!" he cried, radiating confidence. I heard the thing roaring and beeping the next hour while he shot up the walls. Another uptick in aggression. If I didn't check that corgi, in ten years he'd be standing in a stubbled field, aiming a rifle at wild ducks.

So Nathan thought his parents didn't listen to me.

He was six; his perspective was skewed. They listened to me sometimes: Nathan was *here* because they'd listened.

Walter at my feet, I sat to browse the latest studies on PubMed. But I couldn't concentrate. Victor and Astrid loomed; seven years of unheeded advice swept through my head. Get a dog. Sell the Chrysler. Go vegan. Refrigerate your syrup. Don't buy cotton. Compost your coffee grounds. Put him in private school. Buy a whole-house water filter. Vacation in Tulum! *Aunt Rose, they don't listen to you.* Then came an annoying question, squawky as a seagull: So why do I keep talking? I couldn't form an answer, only pick at the rotting fish strewn along the beach.

When the hands on the clock approached bedtime, I shut down the Nerf machine and instructed Nathan to shower. Ten minutes later we met in the hallway. He was dripping wet and wrapped in one of my old, raggedy towels, his hair combed back like a greaser. One ear oozed fragrant suds.

"Why didn't you use one of the nice new Turkish towels?"

"Where are you going with my neck brace?" he replied.

We looked at each other suspiciously.

"I just thought I'd wash out the mustard."

"No, no!" He pried it from my hands. "I wanna sleep in it. What else did you do?"

"Nothing. I was just about to tidy up your room because—" A bedroom is a sanctuary, I started to say, but the look on his face stopped me. He got into his pajamas and dove into bed. Walter nosed open the door, and I shooed him out again. For a moment I thought Nathan looked shadowy and sad, but when I inquired, he only said, "We should have got the N-Strike *blaster*, it's sold separately."

Catching my reflection in the round bamboo wall mirror, I thought, I look sallow and defeated. That morning Nathan had feared a grown-up was coming to take Hazel away. But I'd made a mess of things and the thought fell out of his mind. He was happy and cocky now; he knew he had the power to keep her.

Bitterly I drew the drapes and flicked off the overhead light, causing the room to contract from its decent daylit proportions to a small, dark box defined by the bamboo bed in which Nathan rested. I'd chosen the bedside lamp for its charming mushroom shape, and although Nathan informed me it sucked as a reading lamp, its amber light worked well enough to reveal him, small and fragile and alone against the intricate scrolls of the peacock headboard. The sight of him fussing at the poppy-bright bedspread, unaware of the strange picture he made (bruised eye, scratched cheek, braced neck, coiffed hair of an Elvis Presley impersonator), hit me with an ungovernable spasm of pity. An ambush of tenderness and despair.

Did he really feel, when it came to chances for happiness, a ghost corgi was his best bet?

He was a good kid, a wonderful kid, obviously a little on the dorky side, but well within the range of normal.

How had he come to feel so alone?

I plunked down on the bed. Nathan, I told him, voice swelling like the tides, you've met a lot of kids so far—in preschool, kindergarten, first grade—but you must realize: You're only at the beginning of a long, rich, wonderful life.

"Is this from a book or something?" he asked.

On I waxed about his social potential, and the impossibility of predicting what adventures life had in store, jawing on until his lids grew heavy, his eyes closed, and his head would have drooped, but he was wearing that ridiculous brace.

"And anyway who *says* you'll always be a lonely, only child?"

His eyes snapped open. "Did they tell you something?"

"No."

He began to blink. "Really, Aunt Rose?"

"Really. But you must know, your mom's not too old to have a baby."

"Whaddya mean?"

"*You* know where babies come from."

His eyes narrowed. He looked around for an escape, but it was bedtime: Where could he go?

"The birds and the bees," I said as (in retrospect) he lay there helpless. "The dad has seeds, called sperm, that get mixed into a white liquid called semen. The mom has eggs inside her body, in her ovaries. She also has a womb, sort of like a handbag, and the penis ejects— kind of like that Nerf thing—the sperm into the womb. People used to think the womb was a sterile field, but I read a PubMed study about uterine bacteria in giant pandas, and you can bet your boots some major studies on women's handbags will follow. But the main thing is: One sperm—one sperm out of millions—joins up with the egg, maybe during a Mexican vacation—and that's the start of a new baby."

He stared at the ceiling, utterly defeated.

"But we don't have to talk about all that." The back of my knees were slick with sweat. "I'm just saying: Don't assume you'll always be a lonely only child. That's short-sighted. Hazel isn't all you'll have, because one day you might—"

"It's not true. They don't want another kid. They've said it a million times."

Had they told him he was the big mistake they made on the Panama Canal cruise?

"I'm sure they don't discuss it with you, Nathan."

"It's not a secret," he insisted. "Mommy says babies are too much work."

"Does she?"

"Mommy says siblings are overrated!"

"No!"

"Mommy doesn't even *like* her sister."

"Ah, but what about Daddy?" I cajoled, smiling brightly.

As soon as I spoke, I realized my mistake.

There was an awkward pause, we high-fived goodnight, I turned off the mushroom. In the hallway, Walter, who had been waiting, sprang to his feet. I'd paid two thousand dollars, passed a criminal background check, pored over pedigrees, and interviewed five different breeders, so my dog would loyally follow me around the house.

Aunt Rose, do you ever feel lonely?

My whole life.

PART THREE

Chapter 1

To anyone overrun with solitariness, carried away by melancholy thoughts, unable to sleep even after taking five melatonin, I can prescribe no better remedy than a row-and-column spreadsheet program, provided you're adept at the higher functions. Crunching numbers, organizing lists, creating a pivot table—nothing is more soothing to a troubled mind. Because I had a sizable backlog of work at Cultured Cow and no chance of falling asleep, I opened Excel and slowly, methodically, picked my way through the cells. Anything to forget the conversation in the Wevet room. Why on earth had I given him a sex talk? And how could I have been so stupid as to ask: "But what about Daddy?"

I'd seen the words form plainly in his mind: *Daddy doesn't like his sister either.*

For four hours I worked steadily, Walter snoring on the kitchen floor. My head ached, my eyes fizzed, and I made stupid mistakes, but I was reluctant to stop. The kitchen windows were black, and the house was deathly quiet, except for the occasional hiss and clang of a radiator. I was like a mummy immured in the tomb of my work—my busy work! my spreadsheets! my worksheets!

Then my cell phone rang. Without thinking, without looking, the mummy stretched out its hand and answered.

"Rose," said the voice—intimate, breathy, raspy. "It's Nadia Vizcarra Lerkins."

At the sound of her voice, the garments of the tomb fell away.

She sounded huskier than she had on the video, but maybe the video was old. Maybe she had allergies. Anyway she said it was Nadia, so who else would it be?

"Can we get to work right away? You work remotely, right? What does that mean? I don't need to come in?"

"I read energy, Rose. We can work across vast distances and into the past or future. There are no limitations of time or space."

"I know! I watched your video. But where are you in time and space?"

Her physical body was in Vancouver, British Columbia, and her astral body was shuttling between Marfa, Texas, and Yoshino, Japan. Obviously I had no clue what that meant, but I made small affirming noises.

"Have you recently felt down—hopeless or depressed?"

"What?" I closed my laptop so I could focus. "No," I lied.

"Do you have trouble falling asleep?"

"Not really."

"Any recent mood changes?"

"No. I'm a consistently irritable person."

"Do you find yourself fidgeting?"

"Well—"

"Or feeling restless?"

"Sometimes."

"Have your bowel movements changed? Do you crave fatty meals?"

"Why are you asking all this?"

"It's a routine assessment before I initiate spirit removal."

"Oh, but it's not for me! It's for my nephew."

Together we chuckled at the mistake. I didn't care she'd read the intake form wrong. Nadia Vizcarra Lerkins had called. I was giddy and forgiving; a fortress in peacetime, opening all gates.

"He's six years old and she's been attached since Sunday. He's my brother's child. My brother and I used to be close until he went on a cruise to Cabo, where he met a woman who wasn't his type—and bam! All of a sudden he elopes, buys a fancy house, has a kid, professes to no longer like classical music. Do you think *he* could have an attached entity? Maybe something entered him on the ship, or on the dock—"

Nadia Vizcarra Lerkins didn't treat adults without their permission. Since I was guardian to my nephew, that was okay. But my brother, that would be like rummaging through a stranger's pockets.

"He has to invite me into his energy field."

"All right, I get it." And I sort of did. A week ago, I hadn't believed in an unseen world, and now I was parsing the ethics of energetic healing. Clearly I'd crossed over to the loony place.

"I don't track my nephew's bowel habits, but he's definitely changed. He calls her Hazel and he's always talking to her."

"It might be a demon," she said. "Demons tend to be very chatty."

"Is a demon the same as a dark entity?"

"Rose, it would take a lifetime to explain."

"Try me."

"An elite group of lower-level entities is working to overthrow the human race, and they employ demons to intensify fear."

"Oh my *god*." I sunk to the floor and grabbed hold of Walter.

"You can learn about the internecine demon war another time. An entity? That's when a person doesn't want to die, so their spirit roves around, looking for a host. Once they find a vulnerable human—and children can be vulnerable for all kinds of reasons—they attach and live vicariously. Often the dead person misses their hobbies—"

"*This* entity isn't a person. Listen, my brother gets back tomorrow, and the relationship is strained." The word sounded inadequate, like something I'd do with pasta or tomatoes. "I know your website said three sessions, but I need an expedited healing package. If we do one extended session tonight, or two long ones, tonight *and* early tomorrow morning—that would work. Just so the entity's out before they get to my door at noon."

Nadia Vizcarra Lerkins said no.

Just like that. No.

"Come on," I heckled. "Even the post office has priority mail and priority mail express."

"No." No billowy doubts, no conciliatory frills, no I-wish-I-could-but . . . "If a spirit wants to remain on the earth plane, I can't rush her out, Rose. I have to establish contact and build trust."

"It's an emergency."

"You're sincere but misguided."

"What if I pay double your rate?"

"What do you think the entity is?"

"Triple."

"Rose, you're a noodge."

"Noodge! Are you by any chance Jewish?"

"You said she's not a person."

"Or do you know three Yiddish words, 'noodge,' 'verklempt,' and 'schmear'?"

"What is she, Rose?"

I hesitated. "A corgi." It was like emptying out the contents of my filthy handbag, letting her see the crumpled tissues, the dental floss, the broken tampons, the Gas-X.

"The dog? One of those little fox-headed—"

"Maybe a corgi-Chihuahua mix."

"How do you know?"

"My dog killed her." Now hang up, I thought. Or say, I don't work with corgi-killers, you need to muzzle your dog, obviously you need a trainer, obviously you need a therapist, obviously his aggression stems from your aggression.

Instead she said, "Death is a matter of closing one's eyes in this dimension and opening them in another. The eagle has four talons on each foot, which connects us to the four elements, the four corners of the earth, the four seasons, the transformation of four. Isn't it interesting, that winter is the season in which you've been invited to consider the ultimate transformation?"

On she talked in the soothing, husky voice of the tree trunk. Me: *so* grateful she hadn't hung up. Her: so willing to serve, yet unaware I had elephant-size anxiety, and her tranquilizing voice could only dose a meerkat.

"Just tell me—is it a dark entity?"

"I can't tell anything until I go in."

"But from what I've told you so far."

She said she'd "feel into it a moment." There ensued a long pause, in which I grabbed a fork from the dish rack and drove its tines into my thigh.

"In my professional opinion, based on twenty-two years of practicing spirit releasement—and take this with a grain of salt, because as I said, I don't really know anything

218

until I'm in there—but based on what I've seen, and what you've just said, and my hallowed intuition, which I've learned to value over Western ways of knowing, a dead dog is not likely to be a dark entity."

I released the fork. Like a patient who's just been told the tumor looks benign, I began to blubber.

Nadia Vizcarra Lerkins said, "And I can't rush her out, but I'm happy to begin the first session."

Chapter 2

It was late at night. I was not well rested and was beginning to suspect I had poor judgment even when I was well rested. Nathan was a child and Nadia was a stranger. A session? What did that even mean?

"I just feel my way into your nephew's energy field," Nadia said.

"And if he feels you going in?"

"He's not going to feel anything."

I wondered though. What if he woke up while she was doing it? What if he vomited or wet the bed? What if he thrashed around and had nightmares, or was traumatized for life? Had there been studies—?

"Rose, I was trained by a spiritual master."

"Like Yoda?"

"Yoda's a puppet."

I opened the door to the Wevet room and sneaked a peek: sweet mound of trust, snoring lightly. I whispered his name. No response. A little more tentatively, I whispered Hazel's name. Ditto.

"I promise," Nadia said, "when your nephew wakes up tomorrow, he'll want to drink a lot of water, but other than that, you won't even know I was there."

"I want to believe you, but inadvertently I put him through a lot this week."

In the living room, Walter flung himself on the floor. Wracked with indecision, I leaned my face against his side.

"You must be brave," Nadia Vizcarra Lerkins said. "Push your doubts aside—for your nephew's safety."

"Ugh."

"So say all spiritual warriors when they are at the mouth of the cave."

"I just wish I knew it would feel *all right* to him."

Then I got a notion familiar to parents all over the planet—the ones who taste the chili before risking a jalapeno-scored tongue, test the bathwater before risking a scald. "Nadia, can you do me first? Even though I'm normal, can you check out my energy field?"

"I can."

"Does it take long?"

"No time at all."

"And it's no trouble?"

"No more trouble than walking into an empty room. And you'll see how gentle it is."

In a jiffy it was decided. Nadia said she would iron out any wrinkles in my aura, which might relax me. But even if it didn't, I'd feel nothing, and then I'd understand firsthand how painless an exorcism could be.

"Wait, would you be giving him an *exorcism*? Your website said healing and removal."

But Nadia Vizcarra Lerkins was already giving instructions, hot as a ballplayer, swinging bats in the on-deck circle.

Best if you wear loose, nonrestrictive clothing.

Best if you relax.

Best if you stay away from your dog so he doesn't distract you.

Don't do chores.

Turn off your text messages.

Lie down somewhere you're not likely to be interrupted.

Oh, and sometimes the lights flicker, or a drawer slides open, but if that happens, don't panic. It's just energy. No reason to freak.

"How long's this going to take?" I asked, unsure where to place myself.

Walter was sprawled on my Spanish colonial queen (serpentine pilasters, turned bun feet), and the living room smelled like dog farts.

"Just a few minutes."

I darted into the bathroom, spread two Turkish bath towels in the damp tub, and lay down, fully clothed.

"Ready."

Seven years ago I'd hired an incompetent contractor to redo this bathroom. He hadn't squared the corners, he'd left uneven grout. Into these disappointing memories came Nadia Vizcarra Lerkins's gentle instruction:

"Please say your name."

"My name is Rose Cutler." And I'm an alcoholic, I mentally added, just for giggles. Maybe I'd just lie here and count the subway tiles. No, too aggravating. Maybe I'd just close my eyes while she worked. *Was* she working?

"You're doing well, Rose. Take slow, deep breaths."

"You're right. This is no big deal." Longish pause. "Is this it? I can definitely let you do this to Nathan."

"Hmmmm."

"What's going on?"

"Just keep breathing."

"I am breathing."

"Stay calm. I'm feeling around . . ."

"Do you see anything?"

"I'm not clairvoyant. I'm clairsentient and clair-cognizant."

Something she'd failed to mention when she was closing the sale.

"Well, do you know or sense anything?" I asked.

"There's a dark female energy."

"That's me."

She chuckled. "Keep breathing. I want a little more time."

"You said it would take only a *minute* . . ."

"Rose, I need you to stop talking."

"Everyone needs me to stop talking. There appears to be a goddamn consensus—" But just then something skittered over my ankle. A silverfish. I sat up, felt my ankle, studied the tub.

"You all right?" Nadia asked.

"Yes, I imagined a bug." There was no bug.

"Lie back down please. I'm feeling my way in."

"So you can see me? In your mind's eye?" I lay back down. "I mean, how does that even work, if you're not clairvoyant? Are you—"

"I can sense you, Rose."

"Ah."

"And now I can sense them."

A silverfish skittered across my face. I clapped a hand to my cheek—missed it.

"What do you mean, 'them'?"

"I am preparing to address them."

"Address . . . who?"

"The entities."

I started to scramble up, but—

"Come out of Rose Cutler's head!" she said. "In the name of the Highest and Greatest Source, I dismiss all rogue energies!"

Was this a joke? *Entities in me?* Where was the quiet, gentle, respectful tree trunk voice, what was she suddenly shouting for?

A swarm of silverfish skittered up my body. I slapped blindly with both hands and shrieked.

I dismiss you, Nadia chanted, *I dismiss you, I dismiss you!*

Something sat on my chest. Something pinned my arms. Something struck my skull with swift, repeated blows. And then my vision went black.

Chapter 3

Imagine a murmuring as of the sea, the pounding of
breastplates, the grinding of swords in a shower of sparks.
Imagine the purring and yowling of a thousand cats. Imagine a woman who looks exactly like Nadia Vizcarra Lerkins,
as seen in her videos (NadiaVizcarraLerkins.com), clad
in brilliant white armor, standing high on a hillside and
mounting a stately black steed. In the inexplicable logic
of dreams, I stand squire-like at her side, but also crouch
below in the valley, watching her like she's Netflix.

"Nadia, who are we fighting?" says Squire-Me.

No answer. Over the crest of the hill comes the
demon army—a herd of catlike creatures, twisting and
turning, flicking their whiskers, swishing their long tails,
sinuously swarming over the hillside. Most are hairless,
but don't be fooled! Even the fluffy ones are cold-eyed,
fierce, and maniacal. They come in battalions, young and
old, small and large, disporting themselves like flames.

Lance in hand, Nadia advances, slashing left, slashing right. One devil down, two devils down—like she

was born to fight them. But they dodge and duck and clearly outnumber her. Howling, they jump on her back and head and arms. One leaps onto the horse, who immediately rears up in a panic, pitching Nadia to the earth. I see her roll, groan, blink, recover her sword. Then she must fight the creatures on the ground. Eyes ablaze, she slices an advancing demon neatly in two. But look out, behind you! Nadia spins, grabs a fiend by the tail, and sends him flying. Soon the ground beneath her feet is slick with blood and shit and entrails. Nadia is back on her horse, and I am seated behind her, holding her waist, accidentally eating strands of her hair as they blow in the wind. "Don't look!" she commands, but I turn and see a crowd of demons clamoring behind us, scraping, writhing, howling. Nadia spurs her horse and we outpace them and come to a walled city. The demons swarm behind us, I understand we must enter quickly. In the next moment, we drive a battering ram against the city's thick wooden door. The ram is made of logs and shields, bound together with all kinds of junk. Together we heave, even as, atop the castle walls, demons taunt us. They hurl rocks. They dump vats of oil. A furry demon shoots flaming arrows. All at once, the battering ram catches fire. "Keep pushing!" Nadia commands, and I obey but, oddly, notice I am wearing a kilt. Then I look up at the flaming ram and see, amidst the junk, a midcentury table and six matching chairs— and recoil in horror. Finnish icon! Flawless condition!

SARA LEVINE

Eighty thousand on eBay, at least! I move to rescue a chair, but Nadia yells, "Leave it!" We smash through the door and I see before us a tunnel of fire.

"Come on!" Nadia shouts, but thinking about the time I burned myself trying to get a caramelized onion pierogi out of the oven, I fail to move.

"Go back then, Rose! Go back and when you lie awake in your bed at night, Spanish colonial queen (serpentine pilasters, turned bun feet), remember that your healer, a messenger from the light, a conqueror of demons, who has shed her body like a cloak and penetrated the celestial spheres; who has vanquished armies of darkness; who has flown with Brazilian shamans to the sun and the moon and the cave of the peccaries—or would have, except that day the peccaries happened to be out; who has won praise from mahatmas and kahunas, in addition to movie stars, musicians, and athletes; and whose video on Paranormal Healing now has more than five thousand downloads; when you lie awake in your bed, remember that when you reached the tunnel of fire, you deserted her! Go back, Rose. Or come with me—and find freedom!"

Nadia screams and charges through the burning barrier. The sky erupts in thunder, and I am flung to the ground. I feel the cats as they crawl over me, kneading my chest, scratching my legs and arms. One howls and squats to release a stream of shit into my crying mouth.

Then comes the rain. Thunder, lightning. A few more violations and the devils depart, but there I lie, smelling the rain as it mixes with the stupefying odors of blood and cat shit. There I lie, shocked by filth and gore, twitching with each bolt of lightning. The rain drums down.

Chapter 4

A dog is great at sensing a pattern break. Middle of the night and the shower was on. Why *was* the shower on? Walter nosed his way into the bathroom and barked as I lay lifeless in the bathtub, water level rising, my soft and luxurious bath towels blocking the drain. Remember Landseer's *Saved*, where the Newfie pants over a half-drowned girl he's rescued from the sea? That pretty much paints the picture. First Walter gripped my ankle and tried to haul me to safety. Then he lost his grip and dropped me back into the tub with enough force to wake me up, though now I was underwater again, cold water pelting my face. Wake up, wake up, Walter woofed.

Sometimes the lights flicker or a drawer slides open, but don't panic, it's just energy.

Coughing on the bathroom floor, I tried to work out what happened. Had neutral "energy" turned on the showerhead while I lay in a stupor? Or was an army of dark entities bent on my destruction? The vision of Nadia in white armor came back to me, but other sensations crowded it out. My pajamas were soaked, my head ached, and the shower was still running, wasting—as I frequently tell people—about two gallons of water per minute. I turned it off and clutched the dog. Aloof but serene, Walter allowed me to shed tears into his water-resistant coat.

My cell phone was floating. The circuit board was fried.

Pruned fingers. The oven clock said five a.m. How long had I been passed out? I might have drowned in two inches of water and been found by Nathan in the morning! What had happened?

"Nadia?" I staggered back to the bathroom. "Nadia?" I said, hoping she would astral travel and appear in the soap dish. Had she gone into that tunnel of fire? Was that tunnel of fire my psyche? What if she'd died while battling my demons? The world had cracked. What did I know for sure, except that inside I was a battleground of blood and cat shit?

Chapter 5

"What's wrong, Aunt Rose?"

Seven a.m.: I stood at the kitchen window, staring at the barren crabapple. I whirled around to look at him. "Nothing. Are you okay?"

"Yeah. Just thirsty."

We drank water like we'd just finished a marathon. Nathan drank so sloppily he wet his filthy neck brace. Was he okay? He *seemed* okay. I'm the one who had her energy field mugged! What's up with him? I thought as he knocked back a third glass. Then I remembered the potato chips and hot dogs.

Why's your phone in a bowl of rice? he asked. What's for breakfast? What time do Mommy and Daddy get back? Did they text this morning?

My phone was broken, but I knew they'd be there by twelve.

I felt paralyzed, anticipating the blow.

"Knock knock," Nathan said.

"Who's there?"

"Woo."

"Woo who?"

"You're excited to see my parents too! You liked that one. I can tell you liked it! Hazel's getting funnier, right?" He danced around the kitchen, sucking on his pajama collar.

Breakfast was the usual massive affair. Nathan ate scrambled tofu, crispy potatoes, and piles and piles of toast, after which I suggested we play a proper game of chess. It took us half an hour to set up the board, and in between moves he wandered away, asked irrelevant questions, made silly jokes, and pulled on Walter's tail.

"I like presents," he finally said. "But I don't really like chess." He put his hands on the board and nudged it towards me. "Maybe I think this should be your game."

I tried to convince him otherwise.

"Chess is *everyone's* game. It's the game of kings! People play in France, England, India, Afghanistan, China, Japan—"

I felt myself blush and stopped. I am talking to a pencil sketch, I realized, and his lines are solidly inked. If I'd bought the game at Target and included a gift receipt, Nathan could have swapped it for one hundred N-Strike blasters—and he'd be happy.

"You're right," I said.

He smiled with relief. I dropped the pieces into a drawstring bag and stowed the chess set beneath my bed.

We had risen early. Unfathomably it was not yet nine o'clock. We leashed up Walter and walked around the neighborhood, avoiding the park. The sidewalks were clear, and Nathan chattered happily about what he would tell his parents about Hazel. He thought he'd won. I was so depressed I found it hard to speak. My insides were blood and cat shit. Possibly I had killed Nadia Vizcarra Lerkins. As we turned onto my block, I became aware of a Volvo station wagon trailing alongside us, its tires revolving noisily in the slush.

"It's Tommy!" Nathan said.

Jill Bessinger waved from the driver's seat, rolled down her window, her breath immediately visible in the air. She wore a lemon-yellow angora hat topped with an enormous pom-pom. Fox fur? Raccoon? Jill probably didn't know either.

"I'm so glad I found you. We rang your bell and there was no barking, so I thought, Heigh-ho, they must be out walking the dog!"

From the back seat, which contained Tommy and two, maybe three, of his legendary brothers, there issued various shouts and thumps. Walter was eager to say hello and pulled closer. Yesterday he'd saved my life. Today I thought, Can't he possess more discrimination? Nathan too was drawn to the car like a magnet, laughing as Tommy smashed his nose and lips against the glass.

"Is this about the apology?"

"No. Mind if I follow you back to the house?" I must have looked as if I did mind, because she said, "I just don't want to talk in front of the—" and inclined her head towards the kids.

"All right. But no pony rides," I said, inclining *my* head towards Walter.

"Of course not. They can wait in the car. I need five minutes. Hey, Nate, want to hop in?"

We were twenty yards from my house, but Nathan lit up as if he'd been invited to ride the Oriental Express from Singapore to Bangkok. Inside someone socked him in the shoulder, and as Walter and I tramped home, I heard screams.

Was Jill Bessinger hoping to whisk Nathan off to the trampoline park or an indoor soccer match? Alone with her in the hallway, I began to sweat. These were my last three hours. I unleashed Walter and wiped his paws. Two and a half hours. Someone leaned on the Volvo's horn.

"Rose, I love your house." She peered past my shoulder and into the living room, where BE THE ALPHA Post-Its still puckered up the walls. I draped the dog towel over the radiator. "You have such nice things! It's like a *magazine*. I've been wanting to redo our living room, but John says, Don't bother until the boys are grown. They're rough on furniture. Do you mind?" She shucked off her boots and darted into the living room. The silk Louis XV sofa, the Lucite table, the low-slung leather chairs, the identical twin lamps on fraternal twin tables. She loved it all. My Alexander Girard figurines! Where'd I get the credenza, was the magazine rack antique? Were the ceramic elephants mid-century? And the brass planter, the tortoise with a bulging eye, what was the name of the plant growing there?

"Baby's tears. Safe for dogs." I wished she'd say why she'd come. "You can't keep things nice with a Newfie either. Not without a certain amount of vigilance."

The walls were scuffed, and her socks were collecting tufts of dog hair, but she pretended not to notice. "I think you've done a great job . . ."

"Thanks," I said, but with every compliment I felt more like a mummy whose former greatness could be reconstructed only by scrutinizing her wealthy tomb. Weren't the boys getting cold, sitting alone in that car?

"They're fine. The heat's on. But yes, I'm sorry—selfish of me." She padded back into the hall. "Astrid and Victor said you haven't been answering your cell—"

So that was it! Had they been worrying?

"My phone is dead. I dropped it in the bathtub."

Wait till I tell Omar, I thought. Jill Bessinger had been sent to check on me because I'd gone incommunicado for five days, when my brother had been incommunicado for seven years! The irony was so delicious I started to smile. Walter let out a ringing bark and nudged Jill's belly with his nose.

"You can tell Victor and Astrid we're alive. He's friendly," I added, as Walter fetched a chew toy and flung it at Jill's feet. His tail wagged as he nosed her again, asking to play. But it dawned on me, sort of slowly, as she shuffled into the wall, her lips pursed, making quiet heh-heh-heh noises, that Jill Bessinger was scared.

"*Hold* on!"

I shut Walter in the kitchen and got a tea towel.

"Thanks." Jill dabbed at her coat. "Actually, I didn't come to check on you, I came to— Does he always drool this much? Lemon essential oil helps with anxiety. I came to tell you—but then I got distracted by that paint color. On the baseboards? It's not snow-white, it's not extra white—"

"It's called mascarpone."

"Love it. Well, Rose, I just hate to be the bearer of bad news."

Silence. You could have heard a pin drop. Actually, you could have heard Walter in the kitchen, licking his privates.

My mind went into overdrive: Shot in some Mexican-gang-related crossfire. Drowned in a mat of sargassum. Killed by high winds while trying to unsuccessfully adjust a beach umbrella. Plane crash? Had their plane left already?

My brother died ten different deaths before I heard another word Jill was saying. What if they were *both* dead? A despicable old wish scuttled into sight—tied to my knowledge of a legal document they'd drawn up at Nathan's birth, granting me, in the case of their mutual demise, sole custody; a wish as sub-rosa as they come. No—no more, please—no, just no—

"Don't worry," Jill Bessinger said. "Nobody's dead."

Chapter 6

Seated on the Louis XV, gently stroking the satin piping of one of my favorite throw pillows (a whimsical lattice of leafy lemons and vines), Jill explained. But given her haphazard narrative style and the poor quality of information coming from Mexico, I didn't immediately understand. Even with a series of hysterical texts from Astrid to round out the picture, much was left to be learned.

Yesterday, I think? The Cancún beach has been unswimmable—maybe they told you—because of all the muck—the algae—have you heard about it? It's ruining the tourist trade!—Anyway I guess they were running out of things to do so they signed up for this dolphin thing. Swimming with the dolphins. No, feeding the dolphins. You take your photo with the dolphins—they thought it would be a fun souvenir, something to give Nate. He loves animals!— His eye looks better, by the way. Well, better in the way that, before it looks better, it looks worse—Anyway I looked up the website, and it works like this—[grossly naive description of a horrific experience marketed as Shallow Water Dolphin Encounter, in which participants stand on a platform and pay for three photos: one for the kiss, one for the hug, one for the handshake]. No, you're right—they don't have hands—but the website says—I suppose technically it's not a hug or kiss either— Anyway, he and Astrid were in bathing suits, standing on this underwater platform, near a trainer who had a bucket of fish, and one of the dolphins went craaaaazy—No, I *wish* I knew which one! But on the website the dolphins don't have names. There's just photo after photo of them smiling—I never thought about that; I guess you're right; they're *not* smiling; but you know, their faces? Anyway, completely out of the blue, this dolphin goes nuts and instead of taking the fish from the trainer's hand, it drags Astrid into the water. Terrifying . . . just too awful—well, maybe it knocked her into the water? I grew up watching *Flipper* reruns, so I can't bear to—Minutes, I think.—How did she get out? Good question. Victor didn't say. Someone pulled her out. Probably a trainer. I don't think your brother—no, but I'm sure he was in shock—Not a strong swimmer? Anyway—he tried calling but you didn't pick up—I guess your phone was wet—and the who? Oh the boys!—No, it's fine. They have the keys, and abuse the horn, ha ha, but they can't drive—Anyway this awful dolphin tossed her around and bit her leg—maybe trying to drown her? Victor said her legs are cut up, but it could've been worse. Much worse.

Honking. Jill went to the window to check the Volvo was still there. Then she fingered my drapes.

"So Astrid's okay," I said, shocked.

"She's okay. They signed a liability waiver, but the resort is trying to—"

"Hush it up?"

"Make things right. Poor Astrid! And Victor—first he was dealing with Spanish-speaking doctors, then the resort, and the media, and these terrible, harassing activists who've been trying to close down the dolphin swim park for years—"

"I give money to those people."

"You do?" Jill drifted over to the credenza. "I really like these ceramics, Rose. Do you collect them?"

The boys were splayed all over the lawn, throwing snowballs. The youngest Bessinger had fallen backwards into my hydrangea and appeared to be stuck. Jill yelled that his brothers should help him out, which seemed more a matter of principle than necessity. Arms and legs were tugged, the helpers fell backwards on the soggy grass, Nathan shook with laughter. Then he gave a shout and bounded past me into the house. In a moment he returned, beaming and clutching a Target bag. The Bessinger was out of the hydrangea, and the hydrangea was smashed.

"There *was* candy," Nathan said as his arm disappeared inside the bag's depths. The boys lurched towards him, hands open. "But I ate it," Nathan said (never ashamed

of honesty) and, with a superb degree of ceremony, pro–
duced a wrinkled piece of paper and the Husky Boy shirt
(orange/teal plaid), which Tommy received gladly, gloat–
ing. In fact, he tied the sleeves around his neck and ran
around a bit to show the shirt flapping like a cape. Then
he read the paper—moving his lips—and said, as he stuffed
the missive back into the Target bag, "I wrote an apology
too. But it's at home. It's longer than yours. At least two
whole sentences."

No one was offended by this remark but me.

"See you Monday!" Nathan shouted, as the boys
trooped back to the car.

"Kids react in different ways," Jill said quietly. "But
it's his mother, so I'd be prepared for big feelings. I'd stress
that her foot is fine. She didn't drown. Maybe don't even
mention the drowning part. Rose, you'll be fine. Just—
you know—keep it general."

"Thanks for the advice."

"Thanks for the info about that British paint
company."

Soon the boys were in the Volvo's back seat, brawl–
ing over seatbelts. Nathan and I stood on the sidewalk,
ready to wave them off. But Jill rolled down her window.

"I have to ask. Is Nate wearing a neck brace?"

"Yes, he is," I said, "though the universally accepted
term is cervical orthosis."

Chapter 7

N athan bounced back into the house.
"Why'd she want to talk to you? Is Tommy in trouble because he didn't apologize yet? He *said* he wrote me one. Hey, we should start packing!"

I followed him into the Wevet room and watched as he pulled clothes out of the highboy. "Do you want to help?" A folded pile of shirts sailed onto the rocker, sleeves opening midair like crumpled wings. "Aunt Rose, they'll be here soon!"

"They won't, Nathan." He stopped flinging clothes. "That's why Mrs. Bessinger dropped by. Your parents didn't get on the flight this morning."

He turned, eyes shining, face lit up with fear.

"How come Mrs. B didn't tell *me*?"

If he cries, I thought, I might cry, and this was a terrifying prospect—the two of us, on the floor, blubbering—not just for his mother but for all the secret griefs of this world. I dropped to my knees and lamely patted his hand.

"Don't worry. It's okay. They're still coming back—they're coming back tonight."

"But why? Why'd they miss their plane?"

I hesitated. Nathan looked wan and wrongly small, like a T-shirt shrunk in the wash. How could I—?

"Just tell me!"

"Your mother got hurt by a dolphin."

He crumpled. Like an old man he groped to the chair and rocked slowly back and forth, staring at my face the way Walter does when he's trying to understand me, or get me to understand *him*.

Well, that was a mistake. I should have prepared the ground a little. Jill Bessinger was right to warn me. Here comes the shit storm . . .

"What happened?" he demanded.

"It seems a dolphin knocked her into the water, and it—it was just a weird thing, Nathan. Sometimes animals in captivity get aggressive. It bit her foot, but she's safe. Your mommy swam out of there. That's the important thing. She just wanted some time to recover."

His voice was breathy. "Can we—can we call her?"

I cringed. "No, I dropped my phone in the bathtub. Remember?"

Now comes the shouting. You and your stupid phone! I want my mom! I hate you! You're just a babysitter! Maybe he'd hide in a closet or run away.

Still taking it in, he blinked rapidly. "Mommy fought a dolphin?"

"Not exactly fought—"

"She was in the ocean, and it attacked her."

"Yes, but—"

"Mommy fought a dolphin and won." He jumped up, the smile on his face broad and bright as sunshine. "Aunt Rose, they could make a YouTube video about it! How I Survived a Dolphin Attack. Mommy—she'll be famous!"

I stared. "Nathan, a stressed-out mammal in captivity bit her foot. This is not a celebrity opportunity."

He waved his hand impatiently. "It's fine. She's *fine*. Hazel and me feel it. Don't worry, Aunt Rose! Awww, I just wish we could *call* them! Mommy fought a *dolphin*." A cloud scudded by: "I kinda wish you'd told me before, so I could've told Tommy and his brothers!" There was more in that vein—disappointed, like I'd given him fifty bucks, but only *after* we left the store. Soon enough the sun shone bright again.

"Ooooh whee, Mommy survived a dolphin attack! Do you think they got photos?"

I could never compete with Astrid now. And then I thought: Why *am* I competing?

Chapter 8

In consultation with *The Encyclopedia of Animals* ("Dolphins and Porpoises," page 287), Nathan spent the next hour drawing dolphin combat.

I bit my cheek. "As long as you've got the markers out, maybe you want to write that apology to Ms. Shingler. Weren't you worried about getting it done before Monday?"

He shrugged and devoted himself to exuberant battle scenes: Astrid versus narwhal. Astrid versus gulper eel. Astrid versus black-eyed squid.

After lunch—leftovers from the fridge; every last snack from the pantry—he abandoned Art, and the afternoon yawned before us. It was humbling—the extra time, the uncertainty about what to do with it. We walked Walter. We played a few rounds of Boggle. He played alone in the Wevet room and broke the motor of the Nerf N-Strike Disk Shot. Walter stepped up and chased after a chew toy but, after nine rounds, retreated into a nap. By four o'clock Nathan's boredom thickened the air. When he began to recite the knock-knock jokes he expected his parents to cherish, I realized time with Aunt Rose was a piece of chewing gum with the flavor chewed out. Here is what he looked forward to: the moment he'd tell Victor and Astrid everything about the corgi.

That wouldn't happen until he woke up the next morning two miles from me. In his own house, in his own bed.

I proposed to take him to dinner—anywhere he wanted.

"Anywhere?" He lay on the living room floor, picking at his toenails.

"Your choice. Well, maybe not that Mexican place again. But anywhere else. A celebration! Our last night."

He rolled around, mulling it.

"We could even dress up," I suggested, wondering what, for him, would constitute formal wear. A cleaner pair of corduroys, perhaps.

"Aunt Rose?"

"Yes?"

Nathan stopped rolling and lay quite still. "Did the dolphin bite off Mommy's toes?"

"Certainly not," I said with conviction. "Tommy's mom said she didn't even need stitches. And anyway your dad knows all about foot care, and your mom's an old pro! Which foot did she have her surgery on?"

"What surgery?"

"The bunionectomy."

"I dunno what you're talking about."

"Are you kidding?"

Last year there'd been heaps of tedious conversation about Astrid's procedure. She'd limped for months, complained constantly that they overcorrected her big toe. How could Nathan not remember? You're a sponge at that age.

"When she had the bunionectomy. Remember the botched bunionectomy?"

"*I* don't know," he said, like I was dragging up shit from the fourteenth century.

I looked at him narrowly. Never mind Astrid's bunions. If he were shedding memories, how could I know he'd retain any of *our* experiences, the ones I worked so hard to create?

"Did you decide yet about dinner? If you change your shirt, I could make a reservation at Bellisario's, which is Northern Italian—"

"Aunt Rose." He rolled over. "*I'm* choosing."

Chapter 9

Twenty minutes later we stood at the counter, ordering a Quarter Pounder with Cheese, a Chicken Classic, a Filet-O-Fish, a large fry, a Coke, a chocolate milkshake, and an apple pie. That was Nathan's dinner. After studying the menu—which had evolved since my visit a quarter of a century ago—I began to order a Fruit and Nut Salad. Then, realizing it contained yogurt, I stifled a gag and ordered French fries instead.

McDonald's!

"It's a nice one," Nathan said, referring to the dining room remodel. "Daddy says when you were kids there weren't this many booths."

We slid into a table by the window, and Nathan sniffed his food before unwrapping it. All around us people hunched over their trays, eating rapidly. A sign on the wall said LOVIN' EVERY SECOND. NO LOITERING PLEASE. In a wall niche stood three plastic high chairs, ready to ruin the palates of a new generation.

But there was no ambient music, just the beeping of the kitchen machines, and the voices of other diners.

"Nathan." I tore open a ketchup. "I know you want to tell your parents all about Hazel when you see them. But let me level with you. They will not understand."

"Maybe not at first." He lifted the bun of his Quarter Pounder and inspected a yellow tile of cheese with satisfaction.

"And they will be very mad at me."

I watched him bite his burger and wipe his hands on his pants.

"Because I'm looking after you. And they never gave me permission to get you a dog."

"But she's an *inside* dog. She doesn't bark, or shed, or jump, or sling drool. She won't ever take a dookie in the dining room!"

"Walter was on antibiotics that day."

"I'm just saying she's easier."

"That doesn't mean they'll want her. Or *believe* in her."

"Aw, I'll convince them somehow." He plunked three or four fries into his ketchup. "She can tell them something surprising, like she did with Omar. Or like with you, she can show what she *used* to look like." He frowned. "Actually, I think maybe she doesn't do those tricks anymore. Because when I tried to do the FaceTime joke with Tommy's brothers—"

I nearly fell off my chair. "You did what?"

He repeated, licking salt off his lips.

"Nathan, you pinky-promised! The whole time I was talking to Tommy's mother, you were trying to make Hazel show her muzzle? On the lawn where anyone could have walked by and seen a talking, laughing corgi?"

"No, just when we were in the car. And it didn't work," he added softly. "And then this morning I couldn't even feel her! I know some kids *never* get an inside dog, and I'm six and three quarters, so I was trying to be brave. But it was awful. I thought she was gone." He brightened. "But she isn't. She explained it all to me. Hazel's never going to be gone. Her and me are just blending!"

The word echoed in my horrified brain: blending. Like Gotcha Matcha!—that yogurt gone wrong. *All those months making the green-and-white swirl. But when people eat it, they stir it into a uniform muck.* No, please! Call back the product!

"We're like the same person now. I hear her and feel her, but I can't show her to Tommy's brothers. Are you—Aunt Rose, are you crying?"

"I don't want her to blend with you, Nathan," I said hoarsely. "If she isn't distinct from you, how will we ever get rid of her? How will you even *prove* her?"

"Do I have to?"

"Yes—if you're going to tell your parents! If you say you hear her voice, they'll cart you off to a therapist. Kids get medicated for stuff like that. I'm sorry to scare you, but they could put you in a hospital!"

I have never seen a child look so sad. And I was the one who put that look in his eyes. In a McDonald's. Behind him hung a poster that said I'M LOVIN' IT!

"Eat your apple pie," I told him. "Before it gets cold."

Obediently he picked up the cardboard sleeve. In my mind's eye I saw a lumpish boy watching TV in a locked-down rec room. A sullen teenager on a wet sidewalk, muttering and holding a sign that said Plea2e HelP. An angry, shapeless man, my own age . . .

"Hey, that's not the pie," I said. He was sucking the cardboard sleeve.

He spat it out and we sat a moment, each of us lost in a private sadness.

"Okay, let's not panic," I said as he picked up his fish sandwich. What a carnivalesque meal! He'd already eaten the burger, the chicken, and the milkshake. It was like dinner had started over again, which in some weird way was comforting.

I said, "Maybe Nadia *can* get her out. Even if she's blending with you."

"Who's Nadia?"

"But let's say she can't. Say I can't reach her, say she isn't . . . available." Please don't let my healer be dead. "Here's what we do. You keep Hazel under wraps all week. Then on Saturdays when you come to my house, you let loose."

"What?"

"Think how fun it could be. Our secret! Every Saturday you'll talk to her, or feel her, or whatever it is you do, and I'll laugh at all her knock-knock jokes!"

Nathan tucked his chin. "Mommy says we don't have secrets in our family."

"If you want to drag your mother into this—" I snorted.

Of course, his mother had been dragged into it long ago. I was swimming in dark water, emitting a stream of beeps and whistles, trying to clear the obstacles in my path.

"You're gonna say she's never been a dog person," Nathan offered.

"No, I was going to say: Because of that dolphin, this is the worst possible time to tell your mom about Hazel."

"Mommy crushed that dolphin!"

"She didn't *want* to crush it. She wanted to lie around on the beach and nap. And now she's all revved up."

It was dumb luck! He took the idea even farther than I'd imagined.

"You mean, she might wanna fight *Hazel*?"

"Look, your parents aren't as steady as some people, and you and I—we're steady as a metronome. You've never seen a metronome. We're steady as this table, which has a single post and is bolted to the floor."

"I never noticed." He stooped to look.

"Remember the fighting before they went away? How the trip was supposed to help them get along better? Imagine they come back, all rattled about the dolphin incident, and you start flapping your mouth about Hazel."

"I don't flap my mouth."

"Wrong expression. Imagine they're such a mess they go crazy when you talk about her. Obviously you want Hazel out in the open, but you're a peacemaker at heart. Isn't peacemaking one of the Four Fabulous Rules?"

"Be Respectful. Be Safe. Be Ready. Be Caring."

"Okay, well, not exactly. But you know what I mean. Keep Hazel under wraps and keep our family together."

It was a terrible weight to put on a child. Nathan scratched under his neck brace and pinched a French fry until it split in two. All my happiness hung in the balance, and I couldn't read his face. He shifted in his seat, looked at the mix of food and trash on his tray, looked around the room. Abruptly he smiled.

"Knock knock."

"Who's there?"

"Mary?"

"Mary who?"

"Mary Munn!" he brayed.

"That one's *not* funny. Where's the wordplay—?"

"No, over there! On the bench seats."

Chapter 10

"Oh my god." I covered my face. It was her. Nathan resumed eating. "Why are you acting scared?"

"I'm not scared, I just prefer not to deal with her. Remember how dismissive she was of Hazel?"

"Hazel never holds a grudge about anything."

"Come on! How could Hazel forgive Mary Munn the lousy life they lived together? Or is it because you're blended now—and you're doing the forgiving? No, kids always hold grudges. It must be Hazel. Two legs instead of four, access to education and the arts, a more varied diet. Suddenly she's a moral giant, right?"

"Aunt Rose, that's sour." He slurped the end of his milkshake. "Let's go talk to her!"

He bounded over. Gradually Mary's blank face showed recognition, and she nodded, a gesture Nathan willfully overinterpreted.

"Come on over, Aunt Rose!" he called. "Come over! And bring your fries!"

Reluctantly I rose (that's my name) and brought our trays to the adjacent table. Nathan sat down next to Mary on the bench seat. I dropped onto a stool, uneasily facing them both as they plunged into conversation about the Dollar Menu. Which were the best items? Which were the worst? Was anything in life better than four McNuggets for a dollar? For obvious reasons I recused myself and looked around at the other diners, who were surprisingly diverse. Whites, Blacks, Asians, Latinos. Old people, teenagers, families with small children. People like Mary, I mentally added. But there's nobody like Mary. She was so weird, she wasn't even a type.

"Hey kid, you're on my stuff." Mary tugged the corner of her faux-fur bucket hat. Dutifully Nathan lifted his rear, and that compliance gave me a filament of hope.

I whipped open my wallet. "There's a five," I told Nathan. "Can you get more fries?" Alone at our food-strewn tables, I searched for the last stubby arrow in my quiver.

"Mary, you never took Hazel to obedience school, did you?"

"That costs money. No."

"I've got a little problem."

"Seems like you've got a lot of problems." Placidly she helped herself to our ketchup.

"No, I've got a very specific problem. My nephew—"

"Didn't you just poison a bunch of people with your yogurt?"

255

"We had a serious case of *Listeria*, but we're taking care of it. How did you know?"

"Local news."

"Oh."

"Local brand, local news," she said in a singsong voice. Was she drunk? "I pieced your check back together and Googled you, see? And then I found all these stories about you starting your yogurt company."

"Fun reading."

"I didn't read them. I watched a YouTube video where you say yogurt is good for gut health. You sounded pretty worked up."

"I need to take that thing down." It was an ancient video, one I'd made before the conversation about microbes and immunity blew up in mainstream science writing. In fact, one of my big regrets in life, I told Mary instead of asking her about Hazel, was that I'd read some early microbiome studies and magnified them to market artisanal yogurt as the cutting edge of health. I didn't believe dairy was good for people at all, I said as I glanced at the long line in which Nathan stood, clutching my limp five-dollar bill, and yet I kept selling yogurt and pretending to believe it.

"You're a black-and-white thinker, aren't you? I can spot a perfectionist a mile away!"

"I prefer to think of myself as a scientifically literate person with ethical standards."

"Kim was also a perfectionist," Mary said, steering us back to her favorite subject.

"The woman who deserted her corgi? I think not!"

"She was, she was," Mary murmured. Because I feared a fugue state about her ex-girlfriend, I pretended to agree. I don't regret my interest in the microbiome, I said by way of clarification, only the spurious claims I made about gut health and dairy. In fact, I'd promised to take Nathan to the microbe museum in Amsterdam, which might seem silly since it wouldn't open for some years, but I loved the idea of travelling with my nephew, and by that time, the science would be even better. This was probably the most interesting time to be a scientist, because the complex interaction between microbes and their hosts would soon unleash a dizzying new understanding of the entire animal kingdom, I said, as if I were a professor and Mary a graduate student in biology come to ask my advice. Probably the microbiome was the single most exciting discovery since Darwin, I added as Nathan inched forward in the line. I glanced at Mary, who was, unbelievably, tolerating this conversation, maybe because she was used to tolerating all kinds of invasions of her private space, maybe because she wanted to eat my fries. It was a relief to talk, but it wasn't like talking to Nadia Vizcarra Lerkins.

"Do you believe in healing someone's energy field?" I asked abruptly.

"You mean that reiki shit?"

"I don't know what it's called."

"Like where they wave their hands over you and try to heal you and stuff?"

I nodded.

"No, I think that's chicanery." She pointed to the plastic bowl on her tray. "Looky here, I got the Fruit and Walnut salad, but I don't understand how to eat it. Are you supposed to dunk the grapes in the yogurt? Or is it like a salad dressing? You're a yogurt expert."

I shrugged. Tears filled my eyes for my lost healer, for Nathan, and for all I didn't know.

"They used to sell salads in cups that fit in your car holder. Remember those, Rose? McShakers!"

Nose dripping, I cast around for a napkin. Mary passed me one of hers. Not being an environmentalist, she had a pile.

"You're crying because of that dog, aren't you?" She nodded slowly, gravely. "You don't fool me. Listen up, Rose." She crushed her faux-fur hat onto her head and met my gaze like an old friend. "It's okay that she's gone. No one is mad at you. Just don't you waste any more time worrying about dead dogs or that stuff you said on You-Tube. Look around, and what do you see? People chowing down. But all you've got on your tray is fries. Why don't you get a Happy Meal? It might make you feel happier. They'll let you buy it, you know. The toys are three and up, but they don't ask questions."

Why had I thought this mentally disorganized person could help me? She was the worst conversationalist in the world.

"You know how else I know you're a perfectionist? You got this panicked look when you couldn't answer my salad dressing question. Don't *worry* about it. I ate a McFish sandwich long before you guys came over."

I remembered my question.

"Mary, is there anything you could do to make Hazel obey you? If she were still alive?"

"She isn't alive."

"No, but hypothetically—"

"Are you alone a lot? I want you to lighten up." She whipped off the bucket hat and spoke slowly but vehemently, like a keynote motivational speaker. "Your thoughts are a mirror, Rose! You don't have to like your life, but it's easier if you do. Hate on people, and that hate boomerangs back to you. So relax! And forget about Kim and Patty! Wind farms may create birds, but they also kill jobs. Some people live in the shadow of turbines, but it's like what your video said: Everybody's crawling with bacteria. A gal's gotta decide how she's gonna take it. Maybe some of it's good, some of it's bad, some of it you don't even understand unless you've got the kind of money to fly off to Amsterdam."

A shiver went through me. "Mary, you're right."

"I know I am!" But she looked uncertain, even shocked.

"Are you saying the judgment of right and wrong is like the zigzag flight of a bald-faced hornet?"

"I don't know. Am I?"

"Did you?"

"Did I?"

"Sssshhh."

There was a feeling of emptiness. The sand seeped out of the punching bag. The target at which I'd spent a lifetime firing arrows melted. From the kitchen the beeping of the machines sounded almost like music.

Nathan sauntered back, threw down my fries.

"What do you want me to do with your change?" He showed me a palm of coins.

"Keep it."

Mary pulled a flask out of her coat and took a deep swig.

"Anyone want a cup of tea?"

We shook our heads. She clamped on her hat, wove her way to the garbage, and dumped her tray (a gesture that almost toppled her).

"Bye, Miss Munn!" Nathan shouted as the door closed behind her.

The fries were the same fries I'd ordered fifteen minutes before. So how to explain the delicious scent that rose from the cardboard box? I knew those fries required a pesticide so hazardous farmers shun the potato fields for five days after they spray it. I knew those harvested potatoes sat off-gassing in a shelter the size of a football field before they were cut up, coated in chemicals, and cooked in hydrogenated oil.

But oh the smell!

And the flavor! Hot and salty, light and crisp!

In a minute a woman came in and sat in Mary's place. She put a bulky baby carrier on the seat. Only the baby's feet were visible, small socked feet, kicking under the blanket. The woman beamed and softly sang a song in Spanish as she gave the baby a bottle. She caught me staring. Smiled. We both smiled. The machines kept beeping, Nathan kept eating fries, and I felt, for the first time in my life, that I was in a holy place.

Chapter 11

Nathan's black eye was, in fact, red at first—then black, then blue, and gradually faded to a yellowish green. It was almost like a sunset, and that night, after he got into his pajamas, we stood in the Wevet room, and admired his fucked-up face in the bamboo mirror. It wasn't just the eye. He had the cheek scratch, a small abrasion on his forehead from a collision with Walter, and the brace around his neck. I drew the drapes, turned on the mushroom, flicked off the overhead light.

"Will you wake me up when Mommy and Daddy get here?"

"It'll be late."

"Can't you though?"

"No. You can talk to them in the morning."

"Daddy will carry me sleeping to the car," he murmured, more to himself than me. I sat down on the bed.

"Nathan, I know it's been crazy, but it's been a great week."

"It has," he agreed sleepily. "So much happened!"

"And if I don't see you for a while—"

"You'll see me next *Saturday*, silly."

"But just in case—" My voice hitched in my throat. "I love you. You and Hazel both, I guess. The blend."

He smiled, and clumsily I bent over and wrapped my arms around his back. Our first real hug, no coercion, fully accepted and reciprocated.

Out of habit, he still gave me a slack high five. But as I closed the Wevet room door, I felt bubbly and light, like I'd traded my blood for champagne.

Chapter 12

L ike Hazel, my phone wasn't really dead. I retrieved it
from the rice bowl and turned it on, releasing a flood
of missed calls and messages. Victor, Astrid, Jill, Doug,
Victor, Victor, Victor, the media. I found the number
for Nadia Vizcarra Lerkins, but when I called back, I got
no answer. No voicemail. No way to leave a message. I
turned off the ringer and reburied the phone in the rice.

Their car pulled up at half past twelve, but only Victor came to the door. He greeted me tonelessly as Walter,
wheeling, welcomed him back into the fold.

"Nathan has no homework," I said over the barking.
"I gave him dinner and he went to bed promptly at eight."

Victor nodded. His nose was red and peeling. His
eyes looked watery and small. His mouth twitched. It
flashed on me: He was upset about Astrid. I moved him
into the living room with a rush of warmth.

"Sit down. You must be exhausted. The Louis XV?
Or would you prefer a chair?"

"Anywhere." He stumbled to the sofa and collapsed. Walter stopped barking and companionably dropped his weight onto the floor.

"The universe is a vast, inexplicable soup," I said, "and I've been treating it like a bouillon cube."

Victor looked at me as if I'd just spoken Russian. I sat down beside him.

"One minute you're alive, the next you're dead."

He stared dumbly.

"You thought I'd only say, I told you so. Or, Accidents like this are the dark underbelly of the captive cetacean industry. But no—all I want to say is, I'm sorry it happened to you. And glad that dolphin didn't kill her."

Victor hid his face in his hands and shook. He was weeping. Even as I felt embarrassed for him, I recognized it was a tender moment. I remembered my hopes that he and Astrid would go to Mexico, get drunk, and have the fight of all fights and end their marriage. I didn't want that anymore. I didn't even recognize the person who'd wanted that.

When it seemed he might be finished, I asked, "Is her foot going to be all right?"

"Yeah," he gulped. "But wicked bite marks. All up her leg."

I produced a tissue, tactfully looked away as he destroyed it.

"I told Nathan. I hope that was all right."

"Of course. We don't want secrets. Did he take it okay?"

"Like a champ. He was weirdly excited."

Victor eyed me warily. "Well, better than being terrified," he decided and gave a philosophical sigh. "You know, after seven years of marriage, a person can get a little numb. But when I saw Astrid crumpled up—bleeding, cursing, throwing up seawater—I thought, Ugggh, I *love* this woman." He exhaled violently, wafting the crumpled tissue off his lap. Walter, who has a penchant for such things, made haste to eat it. "It was a near-death experience, Rose. Already it's changed—it's changed my whole outlook."

"I can see that," I said, though I thought: Two days? We'll see. Walter energetically shredded the tissue. "Actually, this week has changed me too."

"I want to be a—a kinder person," he vowed.

"Me too!"

"I want to be more patient."

"Me too!"

"I want to take lifeguard lessons."

"Oh. Okay."

"And sue the hell out of that resort."

"Well, you probably signed a waiver—"

"But most of all, I want to remember how fragile life is. And stop getting wound up about minutiae. I don't want to waste any more time sweating the small stuff. For example, you and I don't always agree, but we're still family, right?" I nodded eagerly. "They call it a Shallow Dolphin Encounter, but it turns out we went pretty deep!"

"I can see you did."

"You may think it's cheesy, but I take nothing for granted now. Excuse me while I text Astrid and tell her I love her!"

"It's not cheesy," I said, remembering my hug with Nathan, feeling my champagne blood. "Victor, remember when Mom and Dad died?" He didn't answer; he was thumb-typing. "I never thought about their souls. I never thought, Did they make it to the other side, or are they still here, wandering around . . ." His phone beeped, confirming Astrid loved him too and was sick of waiting in the car. "But souls can get lost." He nodded, jabbing heart emoticons into his phone. "And it would be like Mom, if she had the power, to come into my body and push me around. I mean, really: If I'd started listening to Johnny Mathis after she died, or watching skaters fall in the Winter Olympics, or complaining the community theatre orchestra was out of tune, I'd be suspicious! She was meek and drew energy from other people's incompetence! But even after she died—"

"No." Victor took me by my shoulders. "No, no."

"No what?" (Confused by the fervent tone, as well as the touching.)

"Stop it, Rose. We have to live in the present, not the past. Because the present's all we've got!" He slipped his phone back into his pocket and made to stand. "Where's his duffel bag?"

"In the Wevet room. But this *is* about the present, Victor." Unconsciously using Walter's tongue click command, I gestured him to sit back down. "After Mom died, I still hated her music and hobbies and taste. I never took up Dad's obsessions either, but until this week I didn't realize how lucky I am! God rest their souls, people say, and now I get it. But what about you? Do you feel clear?"

"Was there a topic sentence back there?"

"We had no religious training, Victor, therefore no inkling of what might exist beyond the material world. But life can exist after death. This week I've rearranged all my ideas about the fact!"

He blinked rapidly. "Is this your idea of consolation?"

"Consolation for what?"

"Do you think if Astrid had died in Cancún, this kind of talk would make me feel better? Ach, never mind. She didn't die. Just sometimes the way you approach a subject, I— No, never mind; small stuff. I let it go."

He removed and cleaned his glasses.

"Did you let it go?" I said.

"Yeah." He put his glasses back on, sat forward, head in hands.

"No, you didn't. I can tell."

"It's something else." He hesitated. "I know—well, maybe it's a communication thing—but I would—actually, maybe now's not the best time, but—"

"Just spit it out."

"Jill Bessinger."

"Predicate, please."

"Jill says she stopped by and Nathan was in a neck brace."

"Geez!"

I concealed my annoyance. Hadn't I given Jill the name of my paint company and let her finger my drapes?

"Nathan's neck is in tip-top shape. The brace is just a comfort thing. His Whippy replacement. I had him checked on Thursday and assure you he's fine."

"So you took him to our pediatrician?"

"No, we were driving downstate to the cold plant—"

"Why wasn't he at school?"

"It's a long story—"

"I *know* why. He and Tommy got into a fight on Tuesday and got suspended, which means when we Face-Timed with you on Tuesday night, you lied to our faces."

"Okay, I did. Don't get uptight about it, Victor. On Tuesday I was strategizing—"

"And I called you, Rose. Many times after that. Even before the dolphin. I left you messages."

"You did, but I dropped my phone in the bathtub."

He closed his eyes. Panting, Walter circled the coffee table, tried to squeeze into the space between our laps.

"Remember what you said, Victor. Don't sweat the small stuff? This is small stuff. Maybe if I explain about the corgi, you'll understand."

"I don't want to hear a dog story, Rose." His eyes were still closed. "You let us down this week."

"I did. I'm sorry." Walter's tail accidentally knocked *The Nutter Butter Bible* off the coffee table. I picked it up. "But I've been thinking all night, Victor, and I decided: I'm not going to put any more demands on you. The Saturday visits. Requests for family dinners. It's going to be better now. I won't push or prod or sulk or anything. I know I make too big a deal about your podiatry school tuition. The mortgage. Time with Nathan. But you can build a sandals business in Hawaii, if you want, and I'll help you with it, financially. I'll even happily eat pancakes at the pancake house."

He eyed me warily. "What's the hitch?"

"No hitch."

"There's always a hitch."

The front door creaked open; Walter exploded, as a dog will do when someone pushes into the house at one in the morning, no doorbell, no knock.

"Hello?" Astrid called out.

Chapter 13

S he looked terrible. It wasn't just the track pants and sweatshirt, or even the limp. There was bloat. Haggardness. Hair that was unwashed. She'd come to hurry Victor along, but Victor said that I was apologizing (in the mildly excited tone of someone reporting an unexpected meteor shower) and would I repeat what I said, especially the financial part.

He and I pulled back the dog—"Walter, don't step on her toes"—and Astrid sat down. There we were, the three of us, lounging in my beautiful living room in the way I'd always imagined. Did anyone want coffee?

"We want to go to bed."

"Of course. Well, I won't waste your time."

Out it came: corgi: Walter: Sunday: park. There were verbs, but here, for efficiency's sake, I omit them.

"What?" Victor looked confused, then aghast. "I thought we were talking about the sandals company—wait, what? Walter killed a dog?"

"I called it." Astrid leaned back, slung her feet up on the coffee table. "One hundred and fifty pounds of id. Didn't I call it? I always said."

I smiled. "It's easy to throw punches, Astrid."

"You never trained him. If you have a dog that big, you have to train him."

"How did Walter kill it?" Victor said. "Did you see him kill it?"

"I don't want to get into unsavory details."

"Of course she doesn't," Astrid said. "Listen to him, panting over there like a serial killer!"

"He's panting because he's hot."

"Then turn down the heat. Just don't start making excuses for him." She jerked her head. "Wait, where was Nathan? Was Nathan with you?"

"He was."

"Ohmygod. Ohmygod."

Jazz hands (inadvertently; it was a touch of hysteria). Victor leaned in, whispering, trying to quiet her fussing.

"I want that dog out of the room right now," Astrid announced.

Walter was literally lying at my feet, doing nothing.

"It's the dolphin," Victor said apologetically. "Her nervous system is slightly dysregulated—"

"Either he goes or me," Astrid said.

"I go."

"You?"

"No. 'Either he goes or I go.' Grammar."

"Maybe we could put Walter in the kitchen," Victor suggested.

"That is a bad dog!" Astrid shouted.

Magnanimously I took hold of Walter's collar and put him in the kitchen, because for the first time ever, I felt I had the higher ground. Not the higher ground I'd thought I had, the one that was always crumbling beneath my feet, but—something new. I curled into the armchair and tried to explain.

"What you did just now, Astrid, I've done my whole life. 'Bad dog,' 'good dog.' Desperate, isn't it, the way we put people and things into piles? I'm finally done judging the living shit out of everything and everybody. Those judgmental thoughts—they're *just* thoughts, and I can pick them up and put them down as easily as I take a book from the coffee table!"

I tugged at *The Nutter Butter Bible*, but Astrid's feet were planted firmly on its snow-white cover. I removed my hands.

"You get the point. I always thought my critical edge made me who I am. But tonight I realized it's what makes me unhappy. So I'm letting go of all the judgments, all the finger-pointing, all the self-righteousness. Who am I to say what's good or bad? Some things just *are*. Like this thing that happened with Walter."

"What exactly did happen though?" Victor said.

I shook my head, basking in newfound clarity, the power of holding my tongue.

"Did he jump on it? Bite it? Did the owners even try to save it with surgery?"

"These are the wrong questions," Astrid said.

"I just want some facts."

"Vic, all you need to know she already said. He killed the fucking thing!"

I looked at my sister-in-law—who, after all, was the love of my brother's life and the mother of the child I adored, who was tired, hungover, and bitten into by a dolphin; who had probably drunk instead of eaten dinner on the flight and dreaded, as one does after vacation, the return to the banalities of her everyday life—and I scraped my heart's jar for the last smear of compassion.

Then I said, "The thing is: The corgi didn't die."

Clearly that meant nothing to them, so I cast out a slightly longer line. A soul thing, I explained; a mingling of souls, what Nathan called a blend—though maybe they were stacked, sort of like a soul pancake?—anyway, I said, two souls now lodged in one body—specifically, Nathan's. Who had repeatedly assured me he didn't mind. Remember that old candy commercial? "Hey, you got your chocolate in my peanut butter!" "You got your peanut butter on my chocolate!"

Between them passed some wordless current.

"You know what?" Victor said. "It's late."

"Yeah, it is," Astrid said. "I miss our bed. Rose, did you pack Nathan?"

"Yes, I did."

"Everything's in the duffel bag?"

"Everything."

"Victor," she said as he sprang up. "Check the bathroom—toothbrush and flossers."

"Excuse the towels! I haven't tidied the tub since almost drowning the other night during the exorcism."

Victor sat back down.

Until then I'd been tottering towards the truth, uncertain I'd complete the hike. How long might I have stood on that swaying bridge, clutching its handrail, looking into a dizzying ravine, before—fearing to lose face—I inched back to the trailhead? But when Astrid said, "What exorcism?"—or maybe Victor said it; anyway someone said it—the question pushed me across.

I said more. Not everything, because I was trying so hard *not* to rant, to keep it neat, even epigrammatic. Possibly in my quest for brevity, I swung to the other extreme and leaped, dolphin-like, over a few explanatory details.

"What? Back up!" Victor rubbed his forehead. "Wait, I don't get—"

"Victor," Astrid said in a brutal tone. She didn't look at either of us, just stared at a spot on the ceiling.

"When you say the corgi is *inside*—"

"We're done," Astrid said in a low voice. But Victor went on:

"Are you saying you pitched our child—"

"Go get Nathan," Astrid told him.

"—some imaginary ghost story—"

275

"I can't carry him with this leg."

"—and dragged him out of school—"

"And *stay clear* of that bathroom."

"—so you could experiment with the occult?"

"Stop engaging!" Astrid punched his thigh.

"No!" I cried. "You totally misunderstand. I called a healer—not a mistress of the dark arts—and she never touched, or needed to touch, his energy fields. She only exorcised *me* in the bathtub."

"I can't even . . ." Astrid said.

Of course she couldn't. Neither could he. Whatever sympathy they might have felt at my words was swept away by judgment. Their chests heaved, their eyes raked me over, and suddenly, despite the awkwardness, everything seemed to make sense. All week Hazel had been trying to explain, Nathan had been trying to explain, but I hadn't been in range to hear. Victor and Astrid sat on the sofa, stiff with self-righteousness, stuck in the proverbial mud, and I—even with all my mistakes!—burbled and flowed, clear as a mountain spring.

"You guys, after Nathan went to bed I went back to McDonald's. I'd felt so unexpectedly good there, and did you know they're open twenty-four hours? Walter and I walked there in less than thirty minutes. But only service animals are allowed inside, so I tied his leash to a post in the parking lot, and nobody stole him! Which in itself is a miracle. Anyway he lay right down in the snow (he loves a good roll!), and I ordered a Big Mac which I ate, sitting in the window. The Big Mac was so good I went back and ordered a Quarter Pounder with Cheese. Then fries. In the end, I ordered maybe five things, not including a sundae, and the whole time I just sat there eating and eating and loving it. I was ecstatic, I was in a trance! I must have been there two hours, and all that time nobody accused me of loitering. In fact, one of the workers said, Is that your dog? and gave Walter a vanilla cone. That's how nice they are! By the time I left, the counter people felt like family. Walter and I floated home. There's a beautiful moon in the sky tonight. Of course, he stopped twice to do his business, which was awkward because I was out of plastic bags and that ice cream did not agree with him, but still: Both of us were floating. And then we got to my front door, and I realized I'd forgotten my keys. Not at McDonald's, at home. I'd literally locked myself out. Isn't that funny? So I grabbed a ladder from the neighbors' shed and was all set to break a window—not a big window, but the little glazed one in the bathroom—when I remembered Omar keeps my spare key. So I called him from the top of the ladder, and even though it was Saturday night, and he had plans, Omar—such a good friend!—stopped what he was doing with his new Grindr boyfriend, and both of them came right over. And then we all got back inside and looked at Nathan, and stroked his hair, and it was such a beautiful scene, I was tempted to make a snack, but Peter said, Don't wake him up, and I wasn't even annoyed that a perfect stranger—who by the way has all these weird piercings and a tattooed neck—was giving me advice. I dropped all judgment—and you know who I have to thank for that? That little dog Walter killed. Who maybe isn't even a dog—why put labels on things? She's the dog formerly known as Hazel and now she's part of Nathan. Which I realize, from your faces, is a lot to take in."

"Are you saying you left a six-year-old boy alone in the house for three hours so you could go to McDonald's?" Astrid said.

"Four hours actually. Omar and Peter had to get dressed."

"And you let in a couple of randos who touched my child in his sleep?"

"Not randos! My best friend and his boyfriend."

"Go wait in the car," Victor told Astrid.

"You know what I want to do?" she growled.

"Yes, you have a great left hook. Please go wait in the car."

She stood up, shaking, and Victor urged her towards the door. Clumsily she wrestled with the lock. "I'm done!" she shouted, raising her volume to cover up the mechanical incompetence. "Victor, tell her we're done!" At last she managed to open the door and slam it behind her.

Victor paced the living room. Took off his glasses, wiped them on his shirt.

"I don't know what happened this week, in this house, or in your mind, but these things you've been telling Nathan—these things you've been telling us! They are problems."

"Problems!" I threw myself onto the Louis XV—still warm from their bodies—and laughed.

"Yes, and laughter is not an appropriate reaction."

"Laughter is the cure for whatever ails you. The doctor said!"

"You have a doctor now? Thank god." He dropped into a low-slung leather chair. "I don't think you're well, Rose. I think maybe you haven't been well for a long time."

"It's hard to be well when people are plotting behind your back. Treating you like poison. I suspected as much, but this week Nathan leaked an unkind nickname. So I know you think I'm an ear-bender. And in the porches of your ears I did pour the leperous distilment."

"What did the doctor put you on?" he asked, squinting.

"'Aunt Rant!' he said. 'That's what they call you!' But I no longer seethe with indignation. I let it pass! In the larger scheme, what's in a name? That which we call a rose by any other name—Hazel knows the rest. And why be afraid of a corgi who knows Shakespeare? All this time—I think she might have been catering to my *taste*! Knock-knock jokes for him, and the Bard for me! And Victor, all week I was so afraid—"

"If you needed help, you should have called us."

"Yes, but you were the *last* person . . . If you found out Nathan had a corgi—I thought you'd blame me! And what if you pushed me out? Poor old me! Abandoned again, looking at that unscalable wall of loneliness."

His cell phone buzzed, and he fished it out of his pocket.

"But Victor, I forgive you for texting while I'm talking. Victor, I was *mistaken*. Do I need family to make me feel good, or safe, or whole? I don't, but the more you pulled away, the more I chased. Now I understand. *That's* why I criticized you and found fault with all your choices. Of course, never out loud—"

"Yes, out loud," he said while thumb-typing Astrid.

"I just had so much contempt for your hasty marriage. And your ugly house! And your boorish, uncultured life! Your soft-bellied desire to live in a more temperate climate! I wanted to tell you: You're wrong! I wanted to tell you, Don't fucking move to Hawaii. The winters you hate so much, or love so much, or love to hate so much, are going to warm up thanks to your support of the agricultural meat complex and its reckless destruction of the planet! I thought I *knew* what was right and wrong. But who was I to order you not to swim with the dolphins?"

"You got *that* one right."

"No, don't you see? Nothing's good!" I laughed. "—or bad—but thinking makes it so!"

Roaring, I fell back on the sofa. Time was going so fast. Just five days ago I'd sat here doing a loon imitation while Nathan tried to tell me he had a corgi.

"Nathan knows! He's got a direct line to infinite intelligence."

"I can't listen any longer to your nonsense," Victor said. "I'm getting my son."

"Get him, but don't delude yourself. You'll never control him." I clasped my hands and sang the wail, the tremolo, the yodel. Is there a loon inside of you? Nathan had asked.

"Keep hooting, that's fine." Victor took a few cautious steps. "But no sudden moves. No surprises."

"Of course, why would we stop you?"

"*We*? Are you threatening to sic your dog on me?"

"Walter's in the kitchen. Dozing."

"Don't follow me—either of you—into the study!"

"It's the Wevet room now," I said impatiently and followed him into the hall. "Before that it was the study, and before that it was *your* room, and this was *our* house. I guess I miss those days—"

"It was never my house!" Victor's voice jumped up to a yell, despite his proximity to Nathan's door. "Every day I lived under your roof, I felt like your fucking toy!"

Victor shivered, his face got red and splotchy. But within me a storm had knocked down all the power lines, and everything that had been buzzing and humming fell silent. I felt calm as a dark and empty house.

"Victor, I raised you."

"You didn't raise me! You *arranged* things."

I leaned against the wall and stared.

"Wasted years!" he muttered. "Years just floating on a sea of fear! I thought if I squeaked, the raft would tip over and drown you. Stupid. Because the worst thing had *already* happened."

"You mean our parents? Their souls are safe—"

"You cannot keep holding me hostage, Rose. Playing victim as you boss around everyone in your orbit!"

"You're twisting things." I pressed my palms against the wall. "I had a scary moment in the bathtub where I feared my insides were only blood and cat shit. But I know better now. *Nobody* is blood and cat shit."

"Sure about that?" Victor spat. *Buzz*—went his pocket.

"As sure as I'm sure she exorcised my demons. You're talking tough because you're angry, Victor. But it's okay, I can listen. I'm soaring above the chaos. I've got the eagle perspective now."

"Sure you do."

"I only wish I knew if Nadia were safe." I mastered the impulse to dash into the kitchen and sink my hands in Walter's fur. "I called her seventeen times on the way back from McDonald's. No answer. Why doesn't she answer?"

Victor snorted. "Because she's ghosting you? Educated guess. I don't know who you're talking about."

His face was still blotchy and his hand clasped the doorknob of the Wevet room, a heavy vintage doorknob I bought at auction. For him. For me! For all of us, I guess. So many fingerprints mingled on the knob. *Buzz!*

"If Nadia died in battle," I murmured, "she wouldn't get lost. She would transition to some new form of energy. Like a flower or a tree trunk . . ."

Buzz. Buzz, went Astrid in the pocket.

"Or . . . or maybe she's out there still, energizing, or inside of me, maybe even guiding me in this conversation, telling me what to say."

"Then I hope she guides you to shut the fuck up."

Victor plunged into the Wevet room. The poppy-bright bedspread rustled, Nathan muttered in his sleep. Gripping the back of the rosewood chair, I aimed my hoots into the Wevet, singing again the Common Loon. Who knew—a spider thread of melody might twist its way into his dream!

Victor emerged with the duffel clutched to his stomach. And Nathan, sweet Nathan, still asleep, clung to his father's back. Hearing the kerfuffle, Walter barked from the kitchen. He wasn't a bad dog, even if he'd done a bad thing. Let his voice join the song! He barked his goodbyes to Nathan as Victor fumbled with the door.

"The web of life is a mingled yarn. Separation is an illusion! No one is alone. Why do you and Astrid have so much trouble with simple hardware?"

I twitched the lock. My brother glared.

"Victor, I know I messed up, but I never abandoned him. He was always safe. I just wanted to be his everything, so I was jealous. But I get it now!"

I flung open the door and the cold air rushed in. My brother ran out.

"Separation is an illusion!" I cried to his back. "Did you hear me? Nathan can't be abandoned; *I* can't be abandoned! We're never alone! Not spiritually, not microbially. Never never never!"

Chapter 14

They abandoned me, of course.

I'll be the first to admit those early messages were prolix, but soon enough I perfected a voicemail, small and controlled as the prick of a needle.

"It's Rose. You left his backpack."

"It's Rose. Please call me."

"It's Rose. I'd love to talk."

Nothing.

The rest of February and all that dreary March, I was inundated with details at The Cow. Gotcha Matcha! was discontinued. I reinstated team meetings and, under Doug's leadership, we put together a plan to rebuild the brand. Sylvia Klausner, claiming the office had *always* been toxic, immediately took a job at Al's Kosher Sausage. But everyone else stayed and worked hard. Sometimes during a lull, someone cast me a friendly look and said, "How's

Nathan?" I either shifted the conversation to the new sanitizing system, or—with a pain in my chest—pretended to know.

One Saturday after my calls had, as usual, gone straight to voicemail, I slung the backpack into my BMW and drove to their house. But a cold, tingling feeling ran up my spine. I couldn't intrude, nor could I toss Nathan's valuables onto the porch. I drove off and returned the following Saturday. Again I parked in front, but this time I sat and listened to the adagietto from Mahler 5, hoping someone would come out. For weeks I did that vigil, undetected, and then one day, towards the end of April, as if patience were rewarded, a figure peeped at me from the upstairs window. A little hand, waving.

A week later Victor's lawyer sent a no-contact request.

In May I took the backpack to Rawlings and deposited it in the lost and found chest. I went in the middle of the day, so as not to run into Nathan on the playground, but my nerves still throbbed. Rawlings's lost and found chest contained an astonishingly large heap of coats, hats, gloves, boots, sweaters, water bottles, backpacks, lunch boxes, and umbrellas. There were even jeans. How could a small elementary school look so much like the basement of Filene's?

I saluted Mrs. Marsh. She saluted back, though I don't think she recognized me. I was just another white lady.

Then I told myself, All right, it's done.

* * *

"They might come around one day," Omar said. I appreciate the kindness of that "might."

In June, to plug up my leaky Saturday afternoons, I hired a dog trainer, a thirtysomething woman named Trisha Brewster. When I said I'd trained Walter with voice commands and tongue clicks, she balked.

"You motivate a hound with the time-honored treat called dehydrated beef liver."

"But I'm vegan."

"Who said *you're* gonna eat it?"

Trisha observed us for ten minutes and asked me to sit in the corner. Two sessions later she had Walter sitting, lying down, and staying on command. Now I cross the street when we see another dog or, if we're accosted unexpectedly, have Walter lie down until the dog passes.

Omar thinks it's funny: I never go out without a pocketful of meat.

He's still dating Peter, and sometimes the three of us hang out or go to the theatre. "Please don't go to any trouble," Omar said the first time I had them over for cocktails. So I served oven-baked plantains, guacamole and chips, and a smoky pear margarita, which is a wonderful drink. You prep the rim of each glass with lime juice and smoked salt. Then combine in your cocktail shaker one and a half ounces of pear nectar, one ounce of tequila, one ounce of mezcal, three-quarters of an ounce of lime juice, half an ounce of agave, a dash of bitters, and a thin slice of fresh ginger. Shake, strain, and serve.

Omar and Peter sprawled on the Louis XV and, rather giddily, I put Walter through his new tricks. I felt proud, but Omar guffawed and said Walter was doing a fake sit.

"Like a fake surrender."

"What's a fake surrender?" Peter asked.

"It's when people say, I'm open to the flow of life, and then send you a ten-point memo." Omar smiled over his glass.

"Walter isn't faking. He knows how to sit!"

I held a piece of liver above his nose.

My beloved dog fixed his eyes on the prize and lowered his haunches, but his ass hovered half an inch from the floor. It was a bit of a revelation. I guess I'd never looked that closely.

"Give it to him anyway," Peter said.

That was a fun night, but I don't mean to suggest life is all smoky pear margaritas and laughter. Sometimes my mind gets active as a prairie dog and I build elaborate tunnels underground, room after room of judgment and justification. It turns out eagle vision crumbles as easily as a block of tofu. But I try not to get bogged down with regrets. These things take time, Omar says. Since I had love and worry twisted up like sheets in a dryer, I wonder exactly how much time it will take.

The hardest part is not knowing how Nathan and Hazel are getting on. Has he kept her a secret? Have they blended beyond recognition? Do they know that I miss them? I wonder if Nathan even remembers all the Saturdays that came before our frenzied week.

Where do you feel her, Nathan?

Inside and all over. She kind of moves around.

I will say this: I'm not as scared as I used to be of loneliness. When the hollowness hits, I breathe and make plans. In eleven years, Walter will be gone; maybe I'll have sold The Cow, moved to Paris; the microbe museum will be open, and I figure an eighteen-year-old boy will be easy to find on social media. Not that I plan to message him. I'll handwrite a letter, and there won't be a word about Mahler or chess or any of the old arguments with his parents. I'll just ask if he ever went back to Rawlings and found his backpack. And in case he didn't, I'll inventory its contents:

three No. 2 pencils, of varying lengths; tooth-
  marked; in need of sharpening
a key chain with a red enameled letter N, no keys
  attached
one barely used beveled pink eraser
the worksheet on consonant blends he completed
  in my living room
[well done, Nathan, on *flat, flip, flute*; *plenty, play,*
  and *plug*]
a plastic whale shark figurine, six inches long,
  open-mouthed, forever hunting
half a baloney sandwich, furred with mold, sealed
  in a Ziploc bag
a crumpled yellow photocopy of the Four
  Fabulous Rules
stale goldfish crackers, swimming freely in outside
  pocket
one blue alabaster knight

Acknowledgments

Thanks to all the people who helped me walk the dog: Rebecca Beegle, Eula Biss, John Bresland, Keith Calabrese, Anne Calcagno, Emily Forland, Sally Gaggero, Roxane Gay, David Goldberg, Elizabeth Hart, Todd Hasak-Lowy, Lindsay Hunter, Joanna Jennens, Jim Lasko, Lillian Levine, Stephen Levine, Mara Naselli, Judith Pascoe, Javier Ramirez, Alice Sebold, Lydia Smith, Tria Smith, Carole Steiner, Carlos Treviño, Liz Webler, and Michael Zapata.

And thank you, Chris Gaggero, for dog walks, real and imaginary. I love you. No hitches.